ANOINT THE DAUGHTER

The Dawning of Heroes
Book 2

JEREMY FLAGG

Cover Art by
SEAN CARLSON

For our everyday heroes.

Children of Nostradamus Universe

The Synthetic Wars

Nighthawks

Night Shadows

Night Legions

Night Covenants

Morning Sun

The Dawning of Heroes

Awaken the Daughter

Anoint the Daughter

Ascend the Daughter

Wayward Orphans

Sentinel Rising

Seraph Falling

Chapter One

1942

My name is Eleanor P. Bouvier.

For as long as I can remember, I've seen ghosts. They're not the spirits of the deceased come back from the past. No, they're manifestations of the future. Throughout my youth they tortured me, showing me an unchangeable destiny. Unable to alter the outcome, I lived tragedies not once, but twice. They robbed me of my family and nearly cost me my sanity. I used to be scared of the ghosts.

I'm not scared anymore.

The sound of muffled whimpers breaking through the white noise of New York had become a beacon, a siren's call impossible to resist. Victims walked the streets, cautious of who might stalk them in the shadows. New York City, my home, served as a breeding ground for those that preyed on the weak. While the war raged in Europe, here in the city, we steadily lost to darkened souls of men.

Barely able to call herself a woman, the girl found herself pressed against a brick wall. A man threatened her life. With police serving overseas, the scum of the city had grown bold. The crying halted as she waited for a well-rehearsed punishment. There was no point in resisting and begging for mercy. She hoped for a swift strike and that it'd end as quickly as it began.

I pulled the collar of my shirt over my nose, fitting the mask into place. Pulling my hair back. I had learned men loved to pull at a woman's hair, a sick dominating pleasure I never understood. I slid my hands into my pockets and ground the stick of charcoal between my fingers. When sufficiently blackened, I close my eyes and dragged the soot across my face. The ritual had less to do with looking the part of a hero, and more to do with summoning the fire.

I imagine my hands hovering in front of me. It started with a spark ready to be snuffed out at any moment. I willed the flame to grow, pushing my anger into my palms. My beloved, Edward, had taught me the visualization, forcing me to take ownership of these gifts, of the ghosts. In my mind, the skin along my hands vanished in fire, nearly blinding as it reached a white burn.

I seized control of the future.

The ghosts no longer terrorized—they served me. I watched as my ghost tore itself free from me and walked into the alley, confident and sure. The ghost would be me in a few, brief seconds. Time slowed as I explored the future through this apparition. I couldn't hear, but I must have shouted at the man. He turned, ignoring the woman he threatened. Not him, not exactly. His ghost separated from his body, a version of him that had yet to happen.

His specter mouthed something, surely vile. I applauded myself, standing tall, unflinching as he drew back his fist. I never knew how far I could stray from what the ghosts revealed. Knowing it was about to happen, I assumed the universe took all variables into account.

His ghost approached mine. His right fist lunged forward, and I sped to the left, moving quicker than should be possible. The ghost was me, a version of me who had already watched this play out. If I thought about the logic for too long, it'd make my head hurt. I wanted to make the world a better place. Beating this man would be the first step toward my goal. Until I could end war across the globe, I'd have to settle for back-alley skirmishes.

I hooked his wrist with my right hand and jabbed at his elbow with my left. I didn't need to hear. His inverted arm gave away a crunch and broken bone. I gave him props for attempting a head butt, a tactic that would have sent me reeling. I leaned away, far out of his reach. Then I ended the fight with a cheap shot, a knee to the groin. Men were more than willing to inflict harm, but the moment I impaled their family jewels, they crumbled like schoolyard boys with a skinned knee.

Delightful. I dismissed the ghosts. Everything gained speed and the sounds of New York flooded my senses. I knew exactly the moves to make, the location of my feet and the tactics he'd attempt. The fight was hardly fair. But we each use the gifts we're given.

"Leave her be," I shouted.

He stepped back, letting her recoil from his grip. I wondered what amusing narrow-minded slur he'd go with. He turned, squaring off against me, sizing me up. Her attacker already claimed victory over a battle that had yet to happen. Perhaps if he could see the future, this would be interesting. But today, I wanted to indulge in the sounds of a man crying out in pain.

"What the hell? You look like a joke, a whore coming to save another whore."

"Whore. Predictable." I no longer had reservations, no desire to grant him mercy. If this was how he treated all women, he deserved a ruptured testicle and a broken arm.

"Let's do this." The ghosts never lied. We met, he swung, I dodged, and it ended with his elbow bending the wrong way and him gripping his manhood while falling to his knees. It hardly seemed like a fair fight.

I grabbed the man by the hair, pulling his head back so I could get close to his head. He needed to realize a woman had bested him. I lost count of how many fights I had won, and with each encounter I grew more confident in my abilities. I had done it in broad daylight at first, but realized if they could make out my face, I put people like my roommate in danger. Now, I dispensed justice without a face. He would cower each time a woman gave him a sideways glance, fearful it might be me willing to show him his rightful place.

"I am watching."

I hadn't come up with a catchy tagline like Edward suggested. It seemed a bit too comical to whisper something philosophical or threatening in his ear. I simply wanted him to run back to his master and report that somebody in the city fought for the defenseless.

"Leave." I stood behind him and pushed with my foot. He scrambled to his knees, hobbling from the alley. Would he lie and say it was a group of men who threatened to kill him? Would I be erased from history and a new, more intimidating narrative be written? Part of me mourned the potential for fame, but only because I wanted the city to know it had a protector who would always do right by it.

"Are you okay?"

The girl nodded. She was obviously far from okay. I had no judgment for her occupation. We each made our choices and had to deal with the consequences. I only hoped she had made a choice and not had it robbed from her. Reaching into my breast pocket, I fingered the bills I hid in case of an emergency.

I handed her several dollars, hoping it would give her a warm meal and a place to stay for the night. "I am watching," I repeated. "Let any who will listen know—The women of New York City have an angel standing watch over them."

She eyed the money, unsure if it was being given or if she'd need to work for it. I didn't wait for an objection or thanks. I needed neither. My heart pounded in my chest, brimming with joy that I left one more creep second-guessing his aggressions.

I walked further into the alley until the light vanished. Only a block from home, I'd needed the walk to unwind. I contemplated lurking in the shadows, going back into the street, looking for another in need. Frank made me promise to keep my evening activities to a dull roar. He feared long nights would give them time to regroup, call friends, or conjure enough bravado to seek retribution. He often reminded me I was gifted, not impervious.

I picked up my pace, wanting to be home before it grew too late. While I was a woman of leisure, I still needed to wake in the morning and work my way through a list of chores. For now, I accomplished one good deed. It might not seem like much, but after countless nights, I hoped the positivity would ripple forward. At least that woman walked away knowing she wasn't alone. One was enough.

For now.

I squeezed the water from the cloth, letting the excess drip into the bowl on the dresser. When I first entered the apartment, I thought Susan Lee might be asleep, but I heard the wind blowing through her window. Admiring the city from the rooftop had become our nightly ritual.

Green eyes stared through charcoal on my face. I admitted it wasn't the most graceful disguise I could muster, but it did enough to obscure my identity. I pulled the collar up over my nose. And just like that, Eleanor Bouvier vanished, and a heroine emerged. I found the power intoxicating. Behind the mask, I became a mysterious vigilante stalking the streets. If the outfit didn't cause hoodlums to stare, then my determination did. A mask meant I could be unmasked. There was a carnal urge, a need to know who hid behind it. Besides the ghosts, the unknown served as my strongest weapon.

I pulled off the jacket and lifted the shirt over my head. Wiping at the charcoal, one pass at a time, I returned. The anonymity vanished, and I stared in the mirror, admiring my bright rosy cheeks and squashed curls. I had spent my childhood hating myself, and only recently, I'd learned to appreciate the woman I had become. The first swipe of the washcloth, I found myself saddened to return to the humdrum of a boring, normal life.

"Boring," I let out a slight laugh, "says the woman who sees ghosts."

With the evidence washed away, only Eleanor stared back. I stopped dwelling on my new identity and hid the shirt, slacks, and jacket under my bed. The last thing I needed was a flustered Susan Lee looking for a blouse to find out I was the woman prowling the streets.

Pulling an oversized sweater over my head, I left my room and went to the fire escape outside Susan Lee's window. I crawled up the stairs and found her leaning on the wall that circled the perimeter. Like always, she held a cigarette, blowing smoke into the air as she looked out over the city. Our apartment building wasn't tall, but it sat in a spot that offered a spectacular view of New York.

"I wasn't quite sure you'd be home this evening," she said. "I thought you might be out with your gentleman friend."

"Edward," I reminded her, "you can call him by his name."

She let out a slight giggle. The giddiness in anyone other than Susan Lee would grate on my nerves. But she somehow managed to be an exception to my rules. "It sounds so much more dangerous to say gentleman friend. Almost like he could be a rendezvous in the middle of the night. A secret lover."

"I think you're projecting, Susan Lee." I liberated her cigarette and took a long drag. I didn't particularly care for the taste, but between the inhale and exhale, I found a bit of relaxation.

"How do you think the boys are doing in Europe?"

I let the smoke roll off my lips, the stream of gray swept away by the wind. "The news says we're doing well."

"Can we trust the news? Sure, they look at the bigger picture. Maybe we're about to win? But what about the soldiers themselves? They will not be the same young men we sent to fight a war."

If I didn't know better, I'd believe Susan Lee had her own gifts. Normally a giddy, positive, and wonderful woman, she had moments of depth that defied her outward appearance. I had to wonder, like me, did she have two sides? Did she hide a radical alter ego capable of plowing through the optimism and seeing the unfortunate reality we lived in?

"They've seen horrible things," I admitted. "Being surrounded by death changes a person."

She didn't ask a follow-up question, an unusual course of action for Susan Lee. Instead, she plucked the fag from my hand and resumed taking deep drags. I leaned on the wall, admiring the beautiful lights that speckled a distant New York. From our perch, the city almost seemed at peace, as if all the awful things had a curfew. I knew better, but from a distance we could pretend.

"And what are they coming home to?"

"How do you mean?"

"You're not this daft, Eleanor. The city is in turmoil. It started with serial killers preying on its citizens. Thankfully, the police solved that problem."

I bit my tongue. The police had little to do with the serial killers stealing mentalists from the street and eliminating them. Hunting those with gifts, they attempted to cleanse the city of these people, *my* people. I have witnessed more than my fair share of death, but until that day, I had never killed. When they threatened Edward and Claudette, the only two I knew like me, I found myself consumed by rage. No, the police had done nothing. It had been my hands that ended that menace.

"But they weren't the worst of it. The rumors about the crime and violence stopped being hearsay. Did I tell you I saw one of those mobsters try to shake down Mr. Kowalczyk yesterday?"

I forced a shocked expression across my face, but in truth, I was anything but surprised. "You don't say? Susan Lee, you need to be careful out there."

"I'm just a poor nurse. They have no reason to hassle me."

I wondered if the girl from earlier thought the same thing? Did she believe herself to be insignificant enough to avoid harassment? Susan Lee could disarm a mugger with a smile, but it didn't mean I worried any less.

"Just promise you'll be careful."

She flicked the cigarette from the roof and cuddled against my side. She rested her head on my shoulder. Again, she broke through my walls and violate my personal space. Susan Lee might very well be the death of me.

"I promise."

"Good. who knows what I would do without you." It was possible to count on one hand the number of people who elicited this level of intimacy from me. I didn't have many friends. I constantly reminded myself to cherish the ones who stayed. They were the family absent from the majority of my life. I would kill for them.

"There's something wrong with the city since they left," she said. I agreed, and it seemed the infection spread more rapidly than any of us anticipated. "Eleanor, what are our troops coming home to?"

I honestly had no answers. There was nobody I could punch or sass. Instead, I wrapped an arm around her shoulders and held her close. Susan Lee proved that not all battles were won by fighting.

Chapter Two

1930

I yelped at the cold, the loudest sound to leave my lips in the last four years.

I had gone from eccentric and imaginative to tiresome and unwieldy. Momma scolded me something fierce, barking at me for claiming Poppa had died. The ghosts had grown weary of torturing only me. I served as the harbinger for their misery. Grief made her cry, but anger had her slapping me across the face. I swore the ghosts wouldn't hurt another person. The only way I knew how to stop them was to commit myself to silence like a nun.

"Are you just going to stand there?" asked Benjie.

Banished from the kitchen, we suffered the cold while Momma napped after her shift at the hospital. The temperature had plummeted the past few days, dipping well below freezing. The house had grown frigid even with a fire roaring, but nothing prepared us for the winter air. With every exhale, I watched the steam of my breath drift in the air before the breeze stole it away.

"You're not going to read, are you?"

I shook my head. Momma understood why I stopped speaking. Benjie, on the other hand, still attempted to catch me off guard. Momma didn't dare explain my refusal to speak. If she did that, she would have to clarify how I knew about the letter from the military before it arrived. Momma feared Satan had latched onto my soul. She didn't want to risk her remaining child.

We walked in silence, putting some distance between us and the house. The snow crunched loudly under our feet, bits finding its way into the tear between the sole and the shoe. My socks grew wet, and I suspected they would bless me with another cold. I wrapped my arms around my torso, hoping to trick my brain into thinking I was warm.

The yard sloped downward, and we were nearly to the massive apple tree we used for shade in the summer. There were hundreds of apples littering the ground, just beneath the snow. Long ago, when the branches were heavy and bending toward the ground making a canopy, Benjie and I played make-believe. Hours would pass until we heard Momma calling our names from the back steps. It felt like a distant memory.

I leaned against the trunk of the tree and pulled my shoe free. I shook it furiously, determined to get the snow out. Once it was emptied of ice, I slid it on, but the damage was done. My sock had soaked through, leaving my toes feeling like little blocks of ice.

"I'm going down to the pond," Benjie said with a flat tone.

Since Poppa had died, his body presented to us in an empty urn, Benjie had changed. He had once seen our father as invincible and a pillar of manhood, but the death left him with a void. Over the years, he grew angry. My brother no longer believed in the principles our father instilled in him. He became increasingly difficult at school and more than once Momma had to leave work because of Benjie's fighting. He hurt, and there was no way to change that.

I felt more out of place each day. I had to wonder if Momma was right and I had a little of the devil in me. Was that why I could see the ghosts while no else could? Even though they only spoke the truth about the future, nobody listened. I caught Momma more than once, hovering in my doorway cursing my name. If I saw the future, why hadn't I saved her husband? Her guilt riddled questions were tame compared to the blame I put on myself. Why? Why hadn't I tried harder?

I spent my days in sadness. It had become the only emotion I experienced. While Benjie transformed into a vessel of rage, I let despair call my heart home. At night, when he had fallen asleep, I lay in bed pondering if these ghosts were a test to prove my determination to survive. The problem wasn't in my determination, it was mistaking that I wanted to go on.

I had no reason to live.

The crunch of snow from Benjie's shoes was far enough away I shouldn't be able to hear them. Once the snow settled on the ground, it was easy to hear footsteps from across the fields. I followed his tracks until I found his patchwork jacket approaching the pond. First I saw him, then I caught a glimpse of his ghost only a few feet ahead of him.

Benjie slowed until I couldn't make out if he was moving or frozen solid. The ghosts, they returned to show me another horrific scene. The resemblance was uncanny, and I had to wonder if the devils conjuring them did it to tug at my heart. Did they want me to see disasters unfold and fear for the person? What did this evil get by watching me endure the pain of the future twice?

My fingernails dug into my hand through the hole in my worn-out mittens. I wouldn't let them see me suffer, not today. I imagined my feelings as a giant blob, and I tucked it away into a box. Just like my vow of silence, I willed a distance from the inevitable horrors they were about to show.

And horrors they showed.

Benjie's ghost stepped onto the ice and almost slipped and fell on his butt. It spun about innocently enough, luring me into a false sense of security. Then it ran a few feet and slid along the edge of the pond. Again. And again. Finally, far from where the frozen water met the ground, he slid one too many times and fell. I held back the chuckle, knowing something horrible was about to happen, something that should send me into hysterics.

The ghost vanished into the ice, hands flailing. The ice itself remained intact, but I could make out mittens waving in the air for a moment before vanishing beneath the surface. I fought back a scream as my ghost ran forward. Running to the water, her arms waved as she approached the ice. She stepped onto the edge of the pond and dipped through the ice. She laid down, shimmying her way onto the frozen surface, but it was too late. The devil had vanished beneath the ice.

Benjie, my brother, resumed his stomping through the snow until he reached the pond. I didn't need to guess, it was about to happen again. Almost slipping, then spinning around, it followed the exact pattern as before. However, this was my baby brother, the boy who shared my bed until two years ago. Today was the day he died. Even knowing the future, the ghosts made sure I was unable to intervene.

I raised my hand and looked through the expanding hole in my mitten. Tiny half-moons bled, staining the yarn. Momma had promised to teach me to knit before Poppa died. After that, there never seemed to be time. Instead, I continued wearing them as a reminder of how much our lives had changed.

Benjie started sliding on the ice. I steadied my breathing, preparing for the moment the ice broke. Each breath brought a shiver as cold air filled my lungs. The slow exhale created plumes of steam that hung in front of my face. The world had a clean smell to it, not quite as fresh as when it snowed, but it was close. For a moment, I almost appreciated winter.

Benjie finished the second slide and started in on the third. The empty spot in my heart, the spot once filled with love and laughter, fought to expand. The memory of Poppa chasing me through the house until he finally snatched me up in a bearhug came to mind. I struggled to remember what his hugs felt like. One of my happiest memories had sullen with age. I imagined someday I would forget his face, just like his fierce embrace.

Benjie slid the fourth time and his arms spun in the air as he fell. The whole pond roared as cracks splintered outward like bolts of lightning. I couldn't save him. My baby brother. I wanted to scream, to tell him to start crawling, I wanted to scream at God. I wanted control over my own life, but I had been placed in the role of victim.

Benjie fell through the ice. I couldn't save him, not now. My ghost showed me running to the edge of the ice, desperate to pull him from the water. I resisted in the only way I could. I stood frozen, watching as arms in a beige jacket waved just above the ice. My stomach tightened, and I feared I might vomit in the snow. I started to look away, to avoid the horror, but I owed it to Benjie to watch.

Tears rolled down my cheeks, and as I struggled to breathe, I could feel the icicles break from my face. Living every moment knowing the horrible future had taken its toll. Even as he prepared to die, I wished it were me. But no, the devil wanted me to continue suffering.

The hole in my chest expanded, an empty space without feeling. I fought against God. I didn't care if he had a plan. He doled out punishment to the faithful, and despite enduring, he robbed me of one of the few things that maintained my sanity. No, if there was a God, he did not understand mercy.

Pond waters calmed and just like that, Benjie vanished. The young boy who helped me slay dragons was stolen from me. The annoying child who always changed the radio dial ceased to be. While I could see the future, I found my mind wanted to reside in the past. I only snapped back to reality when a brisk wind wormed its way inside my jacket.

I couldn't remain a bystander as the darkness attempted to

consume my heart. Just as the ghost had shown me, I ran toward the pond.

The crisp winter air had fallen quicker than expected. The weather mirrored the mood of the house for the past four years, cold and ruthless. Momma had never forgiven me for warning her of the letter that arrived late that night. Without Poppa, she withdrew until she became a husk of the woman who once danced to big band music on the radio.

As I ran, I realized our hearts weren't so different.

Chapter Three

1942

Koji demonstrated the control I craved. His fist drifted through the air, providing me time to make a decision. I swatted the hand out of the way with my wrist and found it had been a distraction for his other hand. Moving at a glacial pace should make fighting easier, but without the adrenaline, and without the ghosts, it served as an exercise, more for the mind than the body.

I batted his hand away with my left arm. I realized the entire routine had been a trap. He quickly grabbed onto both of my forearms and brought his foot to my torso. In a controlled motion, he pulled me close, bracing his heel against my stomach as he fell backward into a roll. In slow motion it hurt even more, being pulled over him and then hurled into the air so I landed on my back.

"Ooph." The ceiling of the gym was lined with rafters. If you stared long enough, they made a beautiful crisscross pattern. I spent enough time lying on my back because of Koji, desperately trying to grasp at air, admiring the construction more than once.

He remained on his back. For such a small man, I found it difficult to believe he could toss me back and forth. But here I lay, again. I had lost count of how many times he'd tossed me to the mats when I made an incorrect decision. Today it had been four. My body would relive each instance when I crawled into bed tonight.

"The distracted fighter leaves no room for error." Koji had a thousand sayings about focus, fighting, and life in general. I wonder if he believed in each of them or he just slapped me with whichever one I ignored. "The watchful fighter opens the door for intuition."

"Right."

"One more time?" I wanted to scream no. I had already spent an hour training with Frank before Koji arrived. My muscles screamed for rest. Covered in a series of ever-healing bruises, I needed to push harder. Susan Lee's speech last night touched something, invoking a fire in my belly. I wasn't sure how it would come to fruition, but I assumed it would involve a clash of personalities. I needed to be the best fighter my body allowed.

"Yes." I rolled over and squared off with Koji. The exposure to kung-fu had been a saving grace, blending the boxing Frank insisted I learn with the centering Gregory demanded I used to harness the ghosts. The cultural lessons were fascinating, but honestly, I learned just how dangerous my body could be thanks to this man.

He offered a slight bow, and I followed suit. As I clasped my hands, I imagined the fire flowing down my arms. Gathering about my fists, I pulled them apart, each holding a flame. When I opened my eyes, the gym was filled with ghosts of patrons that would attend in the next few days. For now, I only cared about one ghost and only a few seconds into my future. Focus, the epitome of this supernatural gift.

I stepped closer, gloves held high, giving away my boxing background. Koji's ghost dipped low, and I recognized the leg sweep. I jumped, his leg passing harmlessly under my feet. He continued with the momentum, standing, using his right elbow to strike my chest. With the ghost displaying his moves before he executed, I knocked his elbow wide and jabbed with my right fist, connecting to his kidney.

I had to keep my ego in check and concentrate on the ghost. With an opponent capable of luring me in, giving me false openings, the ghost provided a warning. With each thrust of his glove, I blocked, dodged, and ducked out of the way. He moved quickly enough I only managed a superficial strike to the stomach. Working out all morning left me weary and fatigued. Koji knew each strike brought me closer to empty.

"Keep your fists up," Frank yelled. I didn't turn, but I knew he had his fists up in front of his face. Those words haunted me at night.

Pushing Koji's knee down, I found the distance between him and his ghost waned. I was losing, and once he caught up, it'd be purely physical skill. I was no slouch, but Koji's style of fighting made him far superior to my boxing. A moment of clarity suggested I adopt more than his philosophy.

Koji's ghost pivoted on one foot, bringing the other leg up in a sidekick that would knock me from the mat. As he executed the move, I dropped, spinning on one foot, dragging the other along until it hooked on his ankle. It wasn't the most graceful sweep, but it caught him by surprise and he toppled.

I fell backward on my butt, unable to continue. Koji's head shot up, a bit of shock written in his thin furrowed brows. He sat up, giving me a quiet clap.

"That wasn't exactly graceful," Frank said. He offered each of us a hand. We faced one another and gave a slight bow.

"Graceful, no," Koji said, "but she is learning to adapt. If only she didn't rely on her boxing so much."

I nearly buckled over laughing. Koji might be the only man in the gym capable of leaving Frank speechless. The small Japanese man might not look intimidating, but he could disarm with his words as quickly as he did his fists.

Frank's lack of retort only fueled the laughter stirring in my belly. "I don't think I've ever seen him at a loss for words. That was worth getting out of bed today."

"Hush," he said.

Koji patted Frank on the chest and went to the bench to pull off his gloves. In the midst of a global crisis, one focused between our people and his, I was glad to see Koji engaged in a gentle warfare with Frank.

"You're getting better," Frank admitted.

"Thanks."

"Ghosts?"

I nodded. "Only for the last match. I'm trying to balance myself. I might not always be able to rely on them," I held up my gloves, "or these. Who knows what I'll need to keep this up night after night."

Frank unlaced my gloves. He didn't particularly care for my recreational activities, but he supported me like a noble guardian. He worried about my safety. Part of coming to the gym to train with Koji and Frank's buddies, I wanted him to see I could handle myself in a fight.

"We had an altercation this morning. Dino decided—"

"Dino is a jerk. I don't know why you let him come back."

"I want to make sure he's still attending meetings. He's been off the booze for almost two months now. But he hates the fact I let Koji practice here."

"Want me to beat the snot out of him?"

"I'm sure being knocked around by a woman would teach him some humility. But let's save that as a last resort."

"Always the peace keeper."

Frank created the gym as a place for veterans to come and reintegrate into society. With a faulty spine, Frank wanted to help other wounded vets make a place for themselves in a world that otherwise discarded them. He was a noble man with a good heart. When the booze became a problem, he found help. Now in the evenings, he offered meetings for those suffering from addiction.

If he wasn't a noble man, Susan Lee wouldn't have been able to steal his gym out from under him. While a boxing ring, weights, and old torn mats occupied the majority of the gym, she had carved out a space for her own project. Unsatisfied with New York's response to the war happening overseas, she'd set up her own makeshift relief center. What started with rolling bandages quickly expanded to veterans knitting socks and mittens. And just when we thought she had reached her apex, she convinced Frank to open the gym for food distribution in the morning. Susan Lee couldn't win the war overseas, but she made sure there was a home prepared to welcome the soldiers back.

I eyed the tables filled with canned food and baskets of vegetables. She solicited donations between managing the center and working as a nurse. She convinced a room full of seasoned soldiers to partake. Converting one heart at a time, she left a path of goodwill in her wake.

"When you see your roommate, tell her she has another ship-ment to send out. And can you please tell her to stop using my office to store her boxes?"

"I think we both know she isn't going to listen to me."

"You and me both," he said. He acted annoyed, but the smirk on his face told a different story. I had seen him at his worst, but underneath the military training, and behind the gruff exterior, Frank was nothing more than a teddy bear with muscles.

"I'll talk to her if you tell Dino I want some words with him."

"Deal," he offered his hand, and we shook.

Frank might not be my father by birth, but he continued to inspire. It had taken years for me to understand our relationship. Individually we were lost souls, but together, we made the other a better person.

"I'll clear out the guys," he headed toward the locker room, "go shower, you smell like a grunt."

Yes, Frank earned the title of father.

I finished patting my hair dry. There was no point in attempting the large curls that was the latest fashion for women. The natural curl made it look as if I didn't understand how to hold the curlers in place overnight. In the gym, thankfully, it was expected that I'd pull it back. But on the streets, I felt like an awkward woman unable to fit in amongst the other ladies.

Sliding my slacks on, I stepped into my shoes. I continued wearing men's fashion for sheer practicality. It was unfathomable how women endured the agony of carrying a purse when pockets were available. I'd need to speak to Emma Jean and start requesting she make me dresses with deep, voluminous pockets.

I froze as I heard shouting from the gym. Heated arguments were common, one man taking a sucker punch from another. Frank believed sorting out their disagreements was part of the integration process. However, the moment Frank's raised voice entered the locker room, I knew trouble brewed.

I hung my towel in my locker, shut it, and turned for the exit. The men had grown accustomed to me, a woman, fighting with them in the ring and spotting them at the free weights. But either they feared my exposed breast or the wrath of Frank if he caught them gawking. The showers always remained empty when I needed them.

I entered the main part of the gym to see Frank standing chest to chest with a man. The men in the gym were leaving their equipment behind, gathering at Frank's back. The dozen veterans were far more fearsome than the three men near the entrance. Frank might not be the fastest man or the best fighter, but I knew in a game of fisticuffs, he could lay out all three of these newcomers.

"If you come into my gym again," Frank jabbed the man in

the chest with a finger, "I promise you won't be able to walk away."

His bark was far more terrifying than his bite, but with a motley crew of former army men behind him, the rumble would only take a few seconds. I crept closer, ready to join the fray if necessary. On the far side, I could see Koji locking eyes with me, nodding his head to indicate we should maneuver behind these goons.

"We don't want a fight," the man said. "We just wanted to make sure you understood that Mr. Bertolucci is willing to make sure nothing will happen to your establishment."

"Nobody here is buying your bullshit protection." Frank swearing usually meant something was about to be thrown.

"That's up to you. But there are unsavory characters that might not be as generous as Mr. Bertolucci. We—"

Frank's fist moved with purpose. His knuckles connected with the man's face, sending blood and spit spraying across the floor. The man reached for his face while the other two men reached into their jackets. Guns. I recognized the bulges hidden under their non-dominant arm.

"Pull them out, and you best hope you can shoot us all before we reach you."

The men hesitated. They pondered their allegiance and willingness to die for the mob boss. It took a moment before I realized I recognized two of the three henchmen. The last time I gambled, they had been the men standing with Bertolucci. Edward had eased his way into their minds and left them docile and ignorant to the fact we walked away with enough money to last the year.

"Long time no see." The man closest to me smiled. I wanted to grind my knuckles into his nose. I held my position. They were far more confident than they should have been in this situation. The arrogance oozed off the mobsters as they held their weapons, prepared to draw them.

"We will be on our way, but please, remember our offer." The man pulled a rag from his pocket and wiped the blood from his lips. He took his time as he folded the fabric, returning it to his pocket. Did he truly believe the horse manure he peddled? Had the mob grown to where they believed themselves untouchable?

"Tell Bertolucci, next time I expect him to do his own dirty work."

The men released their weapons and walked toward the door. The lone man held out his hand, expecting Frank to shake it. When Frank clenched his fist, the man withdrew the offer. "Next time, I'll make sure Bertolucci gives you his personal attention."

Thinly veiled threats didn't rest well with me. The one who recognized me winked as he opened the door. The brazen way they exited had me seeing red, but also left me worried. Were they as brave as they appeared? Was this the underbelly of New York rearing its ugly head?

Frank turned to the rest of the gym. The number of eyes looking to him for guidance had him let out a low growl. Frank didn't fashion himself a leader of men, but here he was, the first line of defense. In a room filled with soldiers, they needed somebody to provide orders.

"We travel in pairs. I don't want any of you on the street alone. If you catch wind of Bertolucci's men sniffing around, you tell me. Do not engage. I have no idea what he is up to, or just how well connected he's become. This isn't our fight."

No, it wasn't Frank's fight. It was mine.

Chapter Four

1942

"You're late."

"By now, I thought you'd be used to it."

The breeze whipped through the park, sending the trees into a violent dance. Branches bowed, threatening to snap under the sudden shift in weather. The humidity had all but blown away and New York returned to a comfortable warmth. I longed for autumn, the cool wind and low temperatures. Unlike the rest of the United States, summers in New York City left everybody grumpy. Pounded by a relentless sun, the pavement proved equally brutal.

"Are you ever going to take this seriously?"

"Gregory." I sat down on the bench next to the finely dressed Scottish gentleman, "If you think my tardiness betrays my serious nature, then I believe you need to work on tuning your abilities."

He sat with his back rigid, bowler hat resting in his lap. To any onlooker, we appeared to be an unlikely pairing. An older gentleman wearing the most formal European fashion, along with a woman who appeared only a step above a vagrant. Thankfully, I came to the park because it offered a respite from the constant barrage of people. I believe it's also why Gregory insisted we meet here.

"How are you, Eleanor?"

"I'm quite fine," I said with a slight nod, "And yourself, Gregory?"

"Do not be coy with me." Like me, Gregory had supernatural gifts that defied the very logic of the universe. Where I could see the future and Edward could read the thoughts of humans, Gregory had the ability to sense the emotions of those nearby. Where Edward couldn't violate the mind of another mentalist without an invitation, Gregory's abilities knew no boundaries. His inability to turn it off was irksome.

"I am processing my feelings right now. I am not quite sure how I feel at the moment. Change is in the air, and for the first time, I feel myself evolving. I have yet to decide if this is a good or bad thing."

"Honesty, Eleanor," he rested a hand on my leg, "it is the hall-mark of our abilities." Gregory had a knack for cryptic speaking. It could take me the rest of the day to see through his wordplay and get to the heart of his words. I wasn't entirely sure if it was just his nature, or if he attempted to be difficult for the sake of sounding wise.

"Unlike other mentalists, you and I are unique. I can hear the emotions of every person. Once upon a time, I would try to inter-pret them, get to the root of those emotions. But I learned specu-lation only muddies the message. Acknowledge your feelings, even if they are a mystery to you. They'll sort in due time, if you let them."

Four months had passed since I met Gregory at this very loca-tion. The portly man had startled me with his ominous message. "They're coming for you." I would have tackled him in that moment, but the softness of his beard, the crow's feet around his eyes, and the gentle manner in which he spoke made him appear harmless. It would be weeks later before I learned he'd used his abilities to subdue me.

"These are turbulent times," he said. "Need I remind you it is surprising that you're alive at all? A child given visions of the future? Ghosts, as you call them. To endure and not give over to despair, you are indeed a strong woman, Eleanor Bouvier."

I dropped my head, focusing on the grass a few feet away. I only survived my childhood by sheer luck. One by one, those I loved had been stolen from me, and this dreaded ability to see the future did nothing to protect me. If I dwelled for long, my chest tightened and my breath grew ragged. I imagined a trunk in my mind, burying the darkness within, I forced it closed and locked away the emotion.

"Incredible," Gregory said. The empath's abilities were always at work, reaching out and grazing the emotions of those around him. He couldn't read my thoughts, but every feeling that passed between my head and heart appeared like ink spilled on paper.

"I am learning," I said.

"Indeed you are," he said. He shifted, turning slightly to face me. "There is pain beneath the surface. I won't speculate or claim to understand, but it's there. What have I been saying since we met, Eleanor?"

Every time he guided me in a meditation to hone my abilities, it came back to a single saying. Without saying it, I could hear his voice in the back of my head. Gregory had been a patient teacher, willing to overlook my stubborn resistance. Under different circumstances, I might have pursued a friendship beyond the boundaries of the park.

"To master myself, I must master my emotions."

He nodded. "You are the sum of your experiences. Yet you continue to lock away the darkest parts of your heart. You've learned to survive and I commend you at this herculean task. But once you can open Pandora's box and accept the worst aspects of yourself, you'll be ready for the next step."

I wasn't ready, not yet. This life I had created, it was the first time I felt comfortable in my own skin. For the moment, I wanted to cling to this bit of normalcy. Eventually, I would face the demons haunting my past, but for now, I preferred to look toward the future.

"Pandora?" I asked, attempting a subtle change in topic.

"Don't think me so gullible." He raised an eyebrow and turned forward, giving me my space. "In Greek mythology, young Pandora opened a jar containing the truths of the world. She released disease, anger, and famine into the world."

"She sounds problematic," I jested.

"But she sealed the jar shut, and only one thing remained inside. Do you have any idea what might have been left?"

Being from a working family and finding myself in the hospital for most of my teenage years meant missing the majority of school. I imagined this might be something taught to students in a history class should they make it to secondary school. I had no idea what might remain.

"No," I admitted.

"While she released the ailments that would plague mankind, she sealed hope within the jar. Hope, Eleanor, the one thing that drives us. Do not lock away your emotions. Buried beneath all your turmoil is hope."

Claudette had referred to me by a Greek name months ago when we first met. She called me Cassandra, a woman able to see the future. But when she spoke, nobody believed her truths. Now, Gregory referred to me as Pandora. I wondered if this was part of the evolution I felt. Was there truth to his words? Beneath the anger and remorse, did hope remain?

"We could speak of myths and philosophy all day. But let's get to business."

"Yes, please." I needed an action I could execute. In the gym, I learned by doing, and I had to assume these abilities were just the same. I needed to practice and the more I flexed my mental muscle, the more capable I would be.

"Do the ghosts still come when beckoned?"

I nodded. Since Edward taught me to summon the fire in my mind, the ghosts had come and gone as I commanded. No longer dogged by the transparent specters, I found they were more acute in their predictions.

"And your visions?"

Ah yes, the visions. Where the ghosts showed me seconds or even minutes into an unchangeable future, the visions showed me worlds unlike anything I had ever seen. I believed they were premonitions of a distant future. But unlike the ghosts, they came and went as they saw fit. To this day, I had found myself inconsistent in summoning the visions.

"They are fewer now. But they come only when they want."

"And have you had any luck with bending the future to your will?" he asked, but his tone suggested he knew the answer. I had an allowance, an acceptable give and take with what I could and could not change. It was less scientific, and I had no clue where the line had been drawn. If I attempted to alter the future too far, it found a way to course-correct. If I saved a man from being killed by a car, it might mean he'd suffer a heart attack moments later. I danced with fate, but she led our waltz.

"Barely." Seeing the future and being bound by these visions caused me the most anguish. "I've tried. At first, small things, moving an object to the left when the ghosts suggest right. But what they deem inconsequential is difficult to predict." The irony of a psychic not knowing the outcome was not lost on me.

"I see." Gregory seldom judged my shortcomings. The man had a gentle nature about him, and I appreciated his willingness to put up with my limitations. In a way, he reminded me of Susan Lee. While she saw the best in the world, he saw the potential in me.

"Sorry," I said.

"No, you have nothing to be sorry for. This is a learning process and one that can take years to master. You have only begun to come into your own."

"But?" I could hear the word hanging on his lips.

"But I fear with those looking for you, you'll need the full extent of your potential to protect yourself. And therefore we continue."

The sensation started at my fingertips and spread through my arms until it reached my spine. I straightened my back, pushing my chest out and squaring my shoulders. A warmth passed through my body and I recognized Gregory's abilities at work. The man weaponized emotion, and with a subtle nudge, he infused me with artificial confidence.

Thankful for the boost, I smiled at the man. "Then, let's get started…"

My head hurt. A dull ache behind the eyes that reminded me that Gregory had no problems pushing my abilities. From predicting the flip of a quarter to testing and attempting to influence the future, he demanded I give my all. Unfortunately, my all usually left me sore in the only muscle I couldn't stretch.

I shifted the bag of groceries to my other arm. I stood on the corner of the street, waiting patiently for the cars to pass. New York had taken on a different tone since the war robbed it of its young men. The city offered an unfamiliar landscape, one populated by women in homemade dresses. While it was more common to see ladies than their male counterparts, there was still an abundance of them as well. Each time I spotted a man, I had to wonder, what prevented him from serving in this war of the world? Were they injured? Did they dodge the military? Or were they hooligans up to no good? The more I prowled the streets at night, the more I became suspicious of men during the day.

I crossed the street, clutching a bag full of produce for Claudette. Much like Susan Lee, the Haitian woman played a role ensuring the survival of New York. Susan Lee worked at the local hospital, while Claudette mended those who would be turned away. Each of us did our part during this turbulent time.

I paused before entering the alley. Looking over my shoulder, I checked to make sure nobody with ill intent followed. A man in a suit holding the newspaper approached, but turned, walking down the street, ignorant to my existence. With a soft exhale, the ghosts appeared, and I ensured that I wasn't tailed.

Darting into the alley, I walked to the end and turned left. Here it widened, large enough for two cars to pass if necessary. Slightly away from the main streets, this allowed Claudette to hide her business from the general population. Only those in need knew she existed, and by all accounts, she preferred it that way.

On the door, a single serpent wound its way around a staff with wings. For a woman who partook in the southern tradition of Vodun, she had made it clear the symbol on the door was for recognition. Hermes staff allowed patrons to know they were walking into a house of healing. However, inside, it housed the most unconventional methods I had ever witnessed.

"Child," Claudette said as I entered, "what goods do you bring me today?"

Our friendship had been born the night I saved her from a psychotic man attempting to eradicate people with gifts. While she insisted her abilities had long since left, I suspected she lied. Since that night, we had grown into a familiar routine. While I trained, I needed mending for the bruises, cuts, and even a broken finger. In exchange for vegetables, she made sure my body remained as strong as my mind.

"I'm certain today's haul will keep you cooking for a few

days." Behind the herbs littering her shelves, I could smell something spicy enough it warmed my belly. The woman introduced me to Haitian cuisine. I learned they were fearless when it came to heat. My mouth watered from the scent of spices.

"But it seems you've already been hard at work," I said as I set the bag down on her counter.

Claudette's shop served both as her storefront and her home. A reception desk sat to the right, but it was the large butcher-block table in the middle that grabbed your attention. Shelves lined three walls, glass jars filled with herbs. Even after months I only knew a handful of their contents. Claudette hadn't seen it necessary to label anything in her shop, just another sign she was far wiser than many might believe.

Behind the counter, there were two doors. One led to a small room with a table where she performed more severe procedures. More than once I had seen bloodied rags littering the floor before she scrubbed away the remnants of a morning appointment. The other door opened into her home, a one-bedroom slightly smaller than the space Susan Lee and I occupied.

"It will be ready shortly," she said, stepping out of her apartment. The woman's skin was the polar opposite of mine, black as the night. She claimed it came from her mother, who was even darker than she. A slender woman, she moved with a fury that betrayed her size. I often wondered if I had not arrived to stop the killer, if she would have been capable of dispatching him on her own. While she only acknowledged being a healer, I believed there was a fierce warrior just beneath the surface. These attributes grew into the reasons I cherished my time with her.

"But until then," she raised an eyebrow at me, "I have a feeling that you are in need of Claudette's services."

She took the bag and set it on the floor by the door to her apartment. Stepping from behind the counter, she gave me a quick inspection. While I could predict the future, and Gregory could read a person's emotions, Claudette claimed spirits spoke to her when she was a child. I hadn't quite figured out how this made her a mentalist the killer wanted to murder, but it was easier to believe than angels hovering over her shoulder.

Grabbing one of the jars, she pulled a sprig of a green leaf free and handed it to me. "Bite down on this," she commanded. She moved from one jar to the next, grabbing handfuls of fresh herbs. I had watched her enough to know that she was preparing a poultice to apply to my bruises.

I bit down on the green leaf and ground my teeth together. As if by magic, the pressure behind my eyes lessened. I would have claimed it impossible, but that seemed to be a blurry line she often defied.

Tossing the herbs into a mortar, she ground them until they were crushed into a fine dust. She added a liquid, stirring it about. Going back to another jar, she tossed in the last ingredient. She never quite repeated the same recipe twice, and I didn't know if she made each concoction tailored to my needs, or if she continued to develop these family recipes.

"Lift your shirt." I unbuttoned my blouse and revealed the purple blotchiness on my sternum. She shook her head. "Child, at the rate you bruise, I'm surprised you haven't broken."

She gathered the salve on her fingers and rubbed it over the bruise in a clockwise motion. As she did, she mumbled a prayer. I tried not to hiss as she touched the sorest spot at the bottom of my ribcage. It took a moment before I realized it matched the sole of Koji's foot. The man landed more blows than he missed, and my body told the story of a slow learning process.

"I hope you bruised him good," she chided. "If you don't whoop his behind soon, I'm going to run out of medicine for my customers."

"I'm getting better." She looked me in the eye, her lips pursed. "It's true! I almost beat him."

"Almost? Like the last time? And the time before that?"

She had a point. "Alright, perhaps I'm just being stubborn."

"Spit," she held up a glass to my lips. I spat out the green herb, suddenly aware my headache had all but vanished.

"You'll be fine, as usual." If Frank was my father, Claudette had assumed the role of my mother. Every time she scolded me for my carelessness, I averted my eyes. But underneath the embarrassment, I silently cheered.

Her hands touched the space just beneath my eyes. She ran her thumbs along my skin, head cocked to the side as she tried to make sense of some unknown. Her hands slipped down to my cheeks, and she gave me a once over.

"You went out last night? Another mission, child?"

Her thumbs traced the lines where I covered my face in charcoal. Again, her supernatural abilities revealed the unseen. Much like Gregory, there was no point in lying or attempting to sidestep the conversation.

"I did. A man assaulted a young girl. He wanted money from her. He didn't get it. I made sure of that."

"Did you do it for her or for yourself?"

"Both." I wanted to protect the girl, but part of me enjoyed the confrontation. As his bone snapped and I kicked him to the curb, I experienced a sense of satisfaction. Part of it due to knowing the streets were safer without him, but the other part was wielding this ability and doing something positive. Yes, definitely both.

"I wish you could have seen it. The ghosts, the fight, it all felt..." I could quite find the emotion to describe the sense of euphoria. I wonder if Gregory had a name for every emotion he experienced? "It felt right."

"You make yourself a target. You know this, right?"

Frank had the same concern. The first time I stopped a mugger in the park, I had done it without a mask. Now that the mob littered the streets, taking advantage of those weaker than them. It became necessary to conceal my identity.

"I'm taking precautions. The mob has no idea who I am."

"It's not them you should fear, child. What if the Society takes notice of a woman wiping out crime in the city?"

I hadn't thought about them when I decided to take to the streets. Frank feared the here and now, guns, knives, and gangs of mobsters. He feared for the tangible threats. Claudette continued to worry about the masterminds behind the serial killer we encountered.

"I—"

"You hadn't thought about them, no? Well, Claudette is reminding you now. Anybody who can make those things is somebody to be feared."

She had a point. "Have you heard anything?"

"No, these days all folks talk about are the men in suits. These men come into our establishments and offer protection, for a price. Those who pay are left alone. Those of us who refuse, well," her eyes rolled back for a moment, "you know how it works."

"Have they come here?" After seeing them brazen enough to enter the gym, I feared they would be lurking around every storefront, including hers.

"They fear Claudette. They know better than to enter my business and cause trouble. There will come a time when even the mob will need healing. They do not dare threaten me."

I wanted to believe she had the ability to weather the storm, but it seemed the mob had no boundaries. "I haven't heard anything about the Society."

"Gregory still does not answer your questions?"

He claimed I was in danger and that this secret organization was coming. However, he never offered evidence or knowledge beyond that. Having been surrounded by people capable of doing things out of the ordinary had left me wondering how he knew. Was it a vision? Did angels speak to him? Did he have informants?

"No," I answered, "but he and I will discuss it at length soon. I think he owes me answers after being subjected to his training."

"And how goes your quest to challenge fate?" In any other context, with any other person, the question would seem like one of her parables. I could never have this conversation with Susan Lee or even Frank. I appreciated there were people in my life who understood more than just the physical world.

"Fate offers me some latitude, but she still holds the reins of destiny."

"I see," she said. I had answered whatever questions she had. Without missing a beat, she turned, heading to her apartment. "Button yourself up and we can discuss less serious things over some gumbo."

I could hardly remember my mother before tragedy struck our family. I wanted to believe she and Claudette were more alike than not. Concerned and loving, but willing to overlook my oddities. While the streets of New York grew more restless, and fear permeated the sidewalks, inside Claudette's apartment, only warmth and love gained entry.

"I thought you'd never ask."

Chapter Five

1942

"Why thank you, kind sir."

Edward slid the chair underneath me and then sat across the table. With a well-rehearsed snap of the wrist, he unfolded his napkin and placed it in his lap. Since meeting at the gala, we spent most our time together between meals and his apartment. It was not the finest restaurant in New York City, but it was far more upscale than the few I frequented.

Multiple utensils rested on either side of the plate. At first, I had no idea why people needed more than one fork, but as salads turned to appetizers, and then onto entrees, I learned each one served a purpose. In the middle of the table a pair of candles flickered, adding to the romance.

You are looking lovely tonight. Like me, Edward had gifts beyond humans. He could speak directly in my head, an additional little voice whispering inside my skull. With humans, he could push and pull information. With another mentalist, he could only speak to them, unless granted access. Like Gregory, I maintained my walls, keeping secrets to myself.

And you are as dashing as ever. We could go an entire evening discussing philosophy or politics but never say a word. To onlookers, we were a troubled couple incapable of dinner conversation. There was a bit of amusement in misleading the rest of the world, the perk of being romantically involved with one of my own kind.

"How does Susan Lee's operation go?"

At his best, I learned Edward was a charming man, even without mental manipulation. We disagreed on many topics, but at the root, he was a gentleman. Passionate and loving, his smile warmed my heart.

"You know Susan Lee," I said as the waiter placed freshly baked bread on our table. "She has expanded her operation. She not only has veterans rolling bandages and knitting socks, but she's expanded. Now she's included a local food pantry to help those struggling with families. Can you believe it? I still get a kick out of those brutish men cursing as they miss a stitch."

"She has a knack for rallying those around her."

"She's not going to rest until she single-handedly saves New York. I swear, that woman is a force to be reckoned with."

You'd almost think she might be a telepath. He whispered the words in my head. Having nearly died at the hands of serial killers, we had become more discreet in our discussions. We never spoke of mentalists aloud in public. Edward didn't share my apprehension about the Society, but he humored my cautious leanings.

"I believe the next course of action will be to ship her to Germany. What could an army do to slow that woman? I'm sure by day's end there'd be peace."

Edward let out a laugh. He had met her on multiple occasions. It only required a single encounter to know that Susan Lee's compassion was as contagious as whooping cough. It was her that inspired me to venture onto the streets at night. While she nurtured New York City, I would remove its plague.

"And how go your extracurricular activities?"

Edward knew. I hid many things from the man, including the details of my gifts. He believed me to be a telepath like him. But when it came to going onto the street and flexing my abilities, I needed another person who understood my capabilities. Edward believed we were given gifts to use, and he was delighted to learn I was coming into my own.

"Quite lovely." I smiled as I sipped from a glass of water with a lemon wedge floating on the surface. "Just last night I had a meeting with a client."

"Oh, did you?"

I almost giggled at the surreal code we had developed. We could have the conversation mind to mind, but it lacked the lighthearted fun. Instead we spoke in code and allegories, with the nearby tables completely unaware that we spoke about beating the snot out of those who attempted to seize control of the city.

"I found they were overstepping the boundaries of our arrangement. I decided it was time to sever our ties and see him to the door with much haste."

"And how do you feel about it now?"

"You know me well enough, Edward." I gave him a coy smile. "I found the exchange to be quite exhilarating."

He let out a chuckle. More than anybody else in my life, he understood using my abilities to change the world. While we might not agree on tactics or when it was a right or wrong time to use them, he reserved judgment. I loved him for holding his tongue.

"You realize it would be even more effective if we ventured into business together?"

On more than one occasion, Edward suggested joining me. At first, I had thought the idea grand. With his abilities to read the thoughts and intentions of those around us, he'd be able to spot culprits faster than my abilities allowed. He'd find my mark, and I'd be more than capable of rectifying the situation.

The waiter came over, a silver pitcher in hand, and refilled our glasses. "Sir, Madam, are you ready to order?"

Edward said nothing, but the man bowed his head and stepped away as if we had given him our order. Our philosophical differences were significant. He believed humans were there to be our fodder, to serve those above them. He created a caste system with us lording above mankind. I still shuddered at the thought of him murdering the woman controlling the serial killers. With no defense, a lone woman in hysterics, he forced her to kill herself. No, Edward and I would never be partners in this.

"I think you know my answer." The smile faded as I gave him a stern glance. "Going into business with one another would be a conflict of interest. And quite frankly, I enjoy our down time just as it is. No need to complicate matters with business."

As you please. Even with a sense of sadness to the statement, he held his thoughts. The man provided me the latitude to have my own life.

Edward, the next words were something I would never utter aloud in public. *The Society. Have you heard anything through your contacts?*

The man stiffened. I tried not to bring it up often, but I refused to believe we had endured the worst of it. While the hounds hunting mentalists were terrifying on their own, to think they had a master providing them orders kept me up at night. I feared meeting the people capable of stripping away a person's humanity and giving them a single gruesome goal.

Not yet. I have probed the mind of every low-life person who might know. They are a mystery. I am starting to believe you are worried about ghosts.

He reached for a piece of bread. Taking a bite, I could hear the delight rolling from his mind. He nodded to the bowl. "It's divine as always, you should have some. You'll need the energy for your next business meeting."

I'm not letting this go. I pushed the thought at him as I reached for the bread. He believed me worrisome and concerned about a boogeyman who might not even exist. However, I did enjoy the bread.

Taking a slice, I spread a thin coat of butter along the top. Warm, almost hot, I took the first bite. Reminded of why I fell in love, I devoured it like a woman starved.

I will continue asking. But in the meantime, if they're here, be careful, Eleanor.

I focused on stealing another slice of bread, masking the confusion running through my mind. For a man who believed this sinister organization was nothing more than a conjuring of wealthy socialites, why did he heed me a bit of caution? I had to wonder, had Edward's informants revealed something more than he admitted?

"Another evening of business?"

"But of course," I jested.

"And I was hoping you'd spend the night." The smirk turned to a smile and revealed that his intentions had little to do with sleep. With his hair cut short, and the stubble shaved, he had a boyish charm I found irresistible. There was no need to share his intent telepathically, I could feel it. The sensation tied a knot in my stomach and slowly moved lower.

"I do believe I have some time between now and my first meeting."

The waiter arrived, a bag in hand. Inside I could see several boxes holding our food. I raised an eyebrow. Edward knew me well enough. First, we would work up a sweat, and then we'd dine. With a suggestion, the man took the receipt and walked away believing Edward had paid him.

I grabbed another piece of bread before standing. "Let's go."

Chapter Six

1942

Hell's Kitchen earned its reputation. If there was crime to be had, I could find it in abundance in this tiny borough of New York. They had pushed the poor from the heart of the city, fleeing to the outer edges in an attempt to maintain a roof over their heads. Filled with people struggling to get by, they were the perfect target for opportunists.

A quick stop by the apartment and I was suited for the night. Black slacks, boots, and my motorcycle jacket, and I was ready to go on the prowl. I couldn't quite explain it, but each time I zipped the jacket, a sense of power washed over me. It had become a ritual as I prepared to save New York City.

Thanks to Emma Jean, I wore a shirt that appeared nothing more than a turtleneck. Hidden in the folds of the collar, a mask waited to wrap about my face. She suspected I might be up to no good, but after giving her the opportunity to flee from an abusive employer, she stopped asking questions. Because of her, my jacket now hid lock picks, sleeves for throwing knives, and thin strips of metal that made it more difficult to cut my flesh. I was far from unstoppable, but as I touched the charcoal in my pocket,

I embraced the idea of being powerful. Tonight, the underbelly of New York should fear me.

It neared midnight, and the only people left on the streets were potential targets. I tried to walk with a purpose, to make myself smaller, to make myself a victim. Turning the corner, I continued walking past a bar and found several men outside, loitering while they shouted friendly obscenities at one another.

I walked between them, ignoring their whistles and statements of sexual prowess. While they were less than savory individuals, they were not the creeps I sought. I let the ghosts roam free, ensuring that none of the men followed. Other than lewd gestures toward their groins, they remained in place. All at once I felt flattered and disturbed by their behavior. If I didn't have bigger prey in mind, I'd stop and show them I was not a woman to trifle with.

With the ghosts walking free, I caught sight of a man in a tailored suit walking into an alley. At this hour, it struck me as odd. I ducked behind steps leading to a tenement building and watched the ghost's owner hurriedly cross the street. As he passed into the light of a street lamp, I grinned. The man from the gym said we'd see each other again, but I don't think he expected it to be this soon.

I reached for the mask and pulled it tight over my face while temporarily dismissing the ghosts. The charcoal in my pocket broke into bits as I ground it between my fingers. Swiping the black chalk across my eyes, I was ready to unleash retribution on the men who threatened Frank. The moment I thought of them standing in the gym, chests proudly puffed out, the anger balled in the pit of my stomach.

I waited for him to vanish before stepping from behind the steps. I reached into my right pocket and my fingers expertly slid into the brass knuckles. The first night I went out, I found myself slammed against a brick wall under a park bridge. I understood fighting against men meant being at a physical disadvantage.

Attempting brute force had landed me bruised and battered. Training with Koji taught me to use more than my muscles. Fighting an opponent capable of physically besting me required I use stealth, deception, and sleight of hand.

I stepped into the alley. Closing my eyes, I listened. My fists may deliver retribution, but they weren't the only skill necessary when hunting. Footsteps vanished as a door slammed shut. Somewhere in the alley, the goon had gone inside, and I only hoped he vanished to meet more scum. Beating one man into submission paled in comparison to stopping the entire operation.

"Remember," I whispered into the night, "stay calm. Stay centered."

I stalked. Entering the alley, I imagined the flame. It always started with a flicker as the ghosts faded into view. I breathed life into the tiny spark, urging it to grow into a ball of reds, oranges, and blues. I imagined it rolling about the palms of my hands, traveling along the skin and up my arms. Pushing the anger into the fire shifted it to blue and white. Here, the ghosts stopped appearing sporadically. I took ownership of what I did and did not see.

Pushing forward, the alley seemed abandoned. I feared I had lost control until I saw one, then two ghosts exit through a metal door. Their tailored suits gave them away, a uniform for the muscle executing Bertolucci's orders. With a mental nudge, the ghosts vanish into the night. I stomped through the alley, certain I'd enter undetected.

I approached the door and saw it was attached to a larger building with a garage door allowing deliveries in and out of the alley. What might they have inside? Were they running weapons? Drugs? Or perhaps it was a space large enough for the bullies to congregate. I reached for the door, preparing myself.

My ghost stepped out of my body and I pulled at the anger, letting it wash over me. My eyes blurred for a moment as the ghost stepped through the door. Not only could I see the actions of the ghosts, but Gregory had also taught me to travel into the future with my specter. The trick had proven useful on more than one occasion. Now, it provided me an opportunity to take inventory of the men inside and learn where I might hide so I could pick my battles.

The hallway had a door to the right, leading into the garage. Through the glass window, several trucks had their rear doors open, stacked with boxes ready for delivery. However, on inspection, it appeared as if there was nobody inside. Further down the hall, I could see a wooden door leading into an office. I didn't need to see inside, I knew they were seated, talking about whatever gangsters talked about when the boss wasn't listening.

Standing at the door, the frosted glass made it hard to see inside. There were two, no three men seated inside. I watched as my ghost reached for the handle and my hand vanished. I lost my hold on the specter, pushing the limit of my abilities. With Gregory's practice, I had gained this skill, but even now, I was far from mastering it. I had to assume I could see through the eyes of my ghost a minute into the future, but beyond that, I had to rely on my own eyes.

Returning to my body, my hand rested on the metal handle. I turned it, making sure it didn't squeak as I opened the door. I closed it slowly, inspecting the hallway interior. Inside the garage, it proved just as I had seen, empty, almost appearing abandoned. I contemplated pulling one of my knives free and slashing the tires of the vehicles. Perhaps when I finished dispatching the men inside, I'd take the time to make sure their vehicles were unusable.

Soft feet, heel, then toe, carefully placed to prevent the floor from creaking. The walls held war posters, threatening the public. Each one reminded citizens that it was their duty to support this ongoing conflict. If they weren't instilling fear, they were enlisting aid. I found the propaganda being peddled by the government to be in bad taste, but each week, new posters littered the city. Frank tolerated the posters outside the gym, but refused to let kids plaster them inside.

A door on the left remained slightly ajar. Peeking inside, I found an empty bathroom, dirt and grime ground into the tile. The door with frosted glass stood between me and the men inside. I gripped the brass knuckles tightly, preparing for the fight. My heart beat rapidly as adrenaline surged through my veins. I focused on the fire and reached for the handle.

"Don't move," said a voice from behind.

Chapter Seven

1942

"Don't shoot." My voice trembled, almost cracking as I begged.

Click went the hammer of a pistol. I had been focused on the door, on the future in front of me that I hadn't taken a moment to turn around. I found myself trapped, and there was no turning back.

"A broad?"

"Please, sir," I raised my hands. "Don't kill me. B-B-Bertolucci sent me."

"Turn around. Slowly."

The world slowed as my ghost stepped from my body. I forced myself to see through its eyes. It pivoted and there stood a slender man in a purple shirt and suspenders holding a gun pointed at my head. I could see the obscenity form on his lips as he caught a glimpse of my face or lack thereof. His finger eased over the trigger as he decided if he should shoot now or later.

The ghost evaporated, and I spun. Pivoting on my left heel, I whipped about, and my right hand shoved his hand into the air. He pulled the trigger, and the bullet vanished into the ceiling. I caught him off guard, but the ruckus would alert his companions.

I brought my right elbow across his face and punched hard into his gut with my left fist. He buckled over, blood dripping from his lip. I jumped with my right knee, slamming it into his face.

"Who's out there? Jimmy, that you?"

The narrow hallway offered little in the way of protection. I summoned the ghosts, needing to see how best to react in the tight space. A thick overweight man opened the door, a cigar hanging from his lip. The moment his ghost spotted me, he went for the revolver in a shoulder holster. Good.

The ghosts vanished, and I held a dazed Jimmy in a headlock. Reaching behind my back, I slid one of the knives free from the jacket holster. I flipped the eight-inch knife in my hand, holding the tip. As the door opened, I threw, hoping hours of practice paid off. The man's eyes didn't have time to widen as the blade struck him in the throat.

Two men were already crowding the doorway as the fat man fell backward over a desk. They reached for their holsters while their ghosts had already drawn them. They fired repeatedly, and in the tight space, they'd be more than likely to hit something vital. I turned, dragging their pal around, taking him by the collar and standing him upright while I turned sideways behind him.

With each bang, his body jerked. They had no qualms with murdering one of their own if it meant they were safe. Their single-mindedness provided me with a window. I just had to survive long enough to reach it. The body in my hands grew heavy, dead, and unable to stand on its own.

Waiting, I listened for the click of empty firearms. I pushed Jimmy forward, letting him crumple. I thought I'd find satisfaction when I made New York a safer place, when I rid the city of the mob. But the confusion on their faces, a cross between anger and cockiness quenched a thirst I hadn't expected.

They felt powerful when they discovered a woman violated their base of operations. My breasts or hips, something signaled to them I was nothing, not a threat, not a person. However, the moment they found my eyes, the hate radiating outward, they understood I viewed them the same. Nothing. Not human.

The one standing in the doorway, the man from the gym, scrambled to reach for the holster strapped to his ankle. I didn't need the ghost. Bent over, he provided me with an easy target. Three longer strides, I brought my right fist down on his head as he attempted to stand. The metal of the knuckles struck him hard enough his entire body stiffened. Falling to the side, I reached back and drilled his temple with the thickest part of the knuckles.

He slumped, sliding down the doorframe.

"Who the fuck are you?"

The remaining man had backed into the office, raising his fists as if he believed himself capable of winning. I could beat him in a fair fight. He'd believe himself faster, stronger, but he hadn't been in the ring training day after day. He hadn't felt the weight of gloves jabbing him every time he got cocky. No, he was nothing more than a minion given just enough power to feel important.

"I have a message for Bertolucci."

I could have taken him, but Frank had warned me about letting my guard down. The man's shaky fists slowed as his ghost took a step forward. He reached into his pants pocket and pulled out a switchblade. He swiped wide, hoping to catch me across the torso and keep me at bay.

As time resumed, I didn't wait for him to approach. I stepped around the unconscious goon and squared off in the tight space. Narrowing my gait, keeping my hands up, knees bent, I readied myself. I trained with and without the ghosts, preparing for moments like these. I had spent my youth as a victim. The girl vanished the moment they had admitted her to the hospital.

I was many things, but I was not a victim.

He stepped forward, reaching for his pocket as the ghost had shown. I didn't wait for him to fumble about for the knife. I pivoted on my back heel and brought up my leg. My foot caught the man straight in the chest, just as Koji had done to me that morning. The goon had been so concerned with the brass knuckles, he never anticipated that my feet might be the real weapon.

He smacked against the wall. The panels of faux wood lining the office shifted, and a sheet shook loose. The mobster pushed off the wall, ignoring the knife in his pocket and attempting to wrap his arms about me. I crouched low, and with the strength of my legs, and upward moving body, I caught him under the chin with the brass knuckles. His teeth cracked as his jaw slammed shut, bits of white flying through the air.

He staggered backward and tripped over his own feet. As he fell his head struck the desk. He died before he settled on the linoleum. My heart pounded in my chest, my muscles ready for the fight to continue. But the only breathing I could hear was my own. I had bested four men, four horrible men.

The big guy lying on the desk was the only one who gave me a queasy sensation in my belly. The other three had attempted to kill me, and I'm certain he would have done the same. But killing a man before he could muster a defense struck me as cold. I didn't like the feeling of taking a man's life unless my own was in jeopardy.

Pulling the knife free, I ignored the wet sloshing sound. I wiped it clean on his trousers and slid it into the sheath. The carnage, I forced myself to take it in. This had been brought about by opening the door and entering. Blood coated the big man's shirt, still oozing from the gash in his neck. The sense of satisfaction, the euphoric feeling I expected? It was nowhere to be found.

The anger remained, a ball of rage. Did I have a choice with these men? Could I have called the cops and trusted they weren't on Bertolucci's payroll? Had they lived, how many men and women would suffer at their hands? Would shops be destroyed if they couldn't pay a ransom? Would young girls be beaten for a few dollars? No, it had to end this way. Nobody should have to see this. I learned if change was to come, I would have to shoulder this weight.

"Uhhh," the man in the doorway groaned as he tried to sit upright.

I grabbed him by the hair, forcing him to see my face. He was hardly conscious, but that would only make my message easier. My entire life had been about carrying an overwhelming burden. If this is what it took to protect New York City, then so be it.

"Tell Bertolucci, this is my city. Either he closes shop, or I'm coming for him."

I dropped the man and headed toward the door. I knew the task ahead of me would test my determination. It should be terrifying, I should be guilt ridden, but somewhere deep in the back of my head, part of me was excited.

I feared the tiny voice urging me forward.

The jacket laid gently on top of the shirt and pants. I pushed it under the bed with the toe of my foot. As it vanished, I tried to put the image of the dead man behind me. Over the years, many things haunted me. The sight of a man I murdered didn't come close to being the most gruesome.

"That's depressing," I mumbled. It was true. The fact I remained standing, carrying on my daily business continued to amaze me. If another person admitted to a past so wrought with pain, I'd be shocked they survived. Each time Frank wrapped his arms around me and held me tightly, it said, "You're still here." I could do this.

I tiptoed my way to the shower, trying not to wake a slumbering Susan Lee. The pipes rattled as I turned on the water. I scrubbed. Soap coated every inch of my body, trying to wash away the deeds of the night. Under my nails, I found a bit of red and scraped furiously. By the time I stepped out of the shower, I swore I had worn away several layers of skin.

A quick pat dry and putting my hair up in a towel, I found myself in my room. My body longed for bed. Buried beneath the covers, I could pretend the strife of the city was worlds away. But I had promised Gregory I would start meditating before going to sleep. I could have dismissed his requirement, but Claudette had suggested the same. He wanted me to practice, she wanted me to find peace. I could multitask while my body prepared for sleep.

I turned off my bedside light and pulled the covers back on my bed, sitting cross-legged in the center. Resting my hands on my knees, I started with the breathing exercises. In through my nose, deep, allowing my lungs to fill and my chest to expand. Hold. Out slowly through my mouth. I repeated the process, paying attention to the parts of my body moving with each breath. The rise of my breasts, the straightening of my spine, the slight lift of my chin, I noted each subtle movement.

Visions. Once I found a comfortable rhythm, the city fell away and nothing remained but the sound of my breath. My mind tried grasping at images, pictures from the past. I fought to push away the distractions. Clear, empty, darkness, silence. I combatted the cluttered thoughts until the only thing that remained was my breathing and my relaxed body.

I turned my hands over, cupping them in my lap. The flame appeared, cradled in my palms. A tingle passed along my spine and the flame pulsed. For a moment, I believed the imaginary fire existed. The warmth spread across my hands. Unlike summoning the ghosts, I wanted it small, quiet, tempered.

Closing my eyes, I watched as the flame danced. I pulled at the heat, drawing it into my body. Creeping along my arms, I forced the flame to shrink until it vanished. I didn't need the flame to summon the ghosts, but it had become the visual that helped keep them in check.

"You are a special child, aren't you?"

My eyes shot open at the voice. Underneath my hands, I could feel the sheets of my bed, but looking down, they had vanished. The pounding in my chest added to the sudden fear. Even knowing I was sitting in the bed, the world had become dark, obscuring the walls.

"Hello?" she asked.

"Who would leave such a sweet child on our door?"

The sound of a large door slammed shut. I jumped at the bang. For a moment I wondered if this was one of Edward's attempts to pull me into the white room. But it felt different. Something unusual was afoot.

"God has blessed us this day," said the mysterious woman.

The tingle ran along my spine again. Focusing on the sensation, I let it pass into my shoulders and down into my hands. I gasped as the area around my bed transformed into a stone floor. I tried to hold on to the sensation. Raising my hand, I slammed the heel into the stone. The sensation was no longer of the bed underneath me.

Touching the cold stone, my legs chilled as if I had been sitting on the floor. Reaching out, I pushed at the boundaries of the mirage. The stone expanded, and I found myself sitting in an office adorned with multiple crosses. A massive oak desk sat opposite me and I could see the top of a woman's head from my point of view.

"You'll need a name," said the voice.

I stood slowly, curious who was speaking. An older woman in a black gown held a baby, rocking it back and forth. The desk was impeccable, everything sitting in neat piles. In the corner, I caught sight of a Bible.

"A church?" I had yet to master the visions. Instead of showing me what I wanted, they picked random moments in the future. I realized the woman wasn't wearing a gown. A nun. I had never found myself particularly righteous, but I felt dirty spying inside a house of worship.

The child made a cooing sound and the woman's face lit up. The smile was genuine happiness, infectious as I found myself smiling. I stepped around the desk and peered out the window, trying to get my bearings. I wondered if this vision was of particular importance or just my abilities run amok.

"Where are we?" I asked.

"Vanessa," she said. "It means butterfly. Beautiful creatures who start off as tiny caterpillars. They don't look so different from you." The woman ran her thumb along the infant's cheek. "But God made sure that when they wake, they are unique and beautiful. Just like you." The child cooed in response.

Outside the windows, there was only darkness, and despite trying, I couldn't see the world beyond this room. I wondered if it was a random vision, or perhaps something about this room was a calling.

"Nice to meet you, Vanessa." The nun rocked the child back and forth, attempting to put her to sleep. But her tiny green eyes continue staring. I admit, for a newborn, the child was beautiful.

"I am Sister Muriel," said the nun. "God has sent you to me. I have you now, child. I promise we will take care of you."

Sister Muriel, I would never forget the name. When the vision ended, I'd grab my journal and begin writing everything I could recall. I wanted to make sure that someday, if it was important, I'd recall every word. I had to believe the visions were guiding me. To what, I had no idea. I refused to believe this was random.

"God has a plan for you," the woman said. I froze at the statement.

"Are you talking to me?" It was foolish to ask, but I couldn't help but feel it was not meant for the infant.

"You will change the world. Now let's find you a crib and we'll sort this out tomorrow."

I stood next to the woman, admiring the child. I had never given much thought to having children. Most women my age were consumed by marrying their sweethearts and settling down.

Part of me longed for the normalcy, but marrying and having children was the last thing on my mind. I couldn't divide my attention.

"Aha," I said. The letterhead rested in the center of her desk. The vision started wavering, the edges vanishing as I leaned in. Bit by bit, the room faded. I leaned close and caught the address just before the room faded.

My eyes shot open, and I gasped for air. I remained sitting on my bed, my hands clutching the sheets. My heart pounded quickly. I recited the address over and over, determined to not forget. Rolling onto my stomach, I reached for the light, flipping it on and reaching under the nightstand. I pulled out a leather-bound book, a gift from Frank.

My fingers traced over the embossing. I pulled at the leather cord binding it together and flipped open to the next empty page. Scribbling the address in the corner, I started writing. Each detail I could recall poured out in a jumble of half-finished sentences.

The sun broke the horizon before I finished.

Chapter Eight

1931

Margaret screamed when the snow started to fall. Her face would flatten against the glass window and she'd claw at it, as if she might be able to free herself. The screams emanated from her belly, deep, blood-curdling screeches that made Meredith and Pearl cover their ears. Eventually, they'd begin screaming. If I was lucky, the orderlies would remove Margaret and the room would return to its usual sedated state.

"Let me out," she screamed.

It happened in slow motion, Isaac jumping from his chair and running toward Margaret. I knew what came next. The demons made sure I experienced each horror twice. At any moment, Isaac would jump from his chair and charge, screaming in Margaret's ear. Lacking impulse control, he only knew one way to handle negative feelings. With his fingers wrapped in her hair, he'd crack the glass using her as a blunt instrument. The orderlies would charge into the room, but they'd be too late to save poor Margaret.

It unfolded just as the demons had shown me. I watched, refusing to cower. The ghosts showed me events, but it was more

54

unsettling to hear them. Her scream ceased as he smashed her head against the glass, once, twice, a third time. He yelled, imitating her uncontrollable fit. The first orderly pulled him off while he kicked and screamed. Even Meredith and Pearl turned away, huddling together for fear he'd come after them next.

Unlike Margaret, they'd survive. The ghosts hadn't shown Isaac murdering them.

A nurse would eventually hover over Margaret's corpse. They'd drag her onto a gurney. They wouldn't rush to remove her from the room where twenty men and women in white cotton gowns stared in horror. I didn't know why it came as a shock anymore, not here in this home for the damned.

"Did you see what happened?" The orderly looked at me, but I continued staring out the window to watch the snow.

"Hey," he said loudly, "I'm talking to you."

I made no attempt to engage. The snow drifted down quickly enough to leave little piles on the window sill. He lunged, not threatening to attack, but hoping he could get a rise out of me. I lived in constant fear. The demons determined to drive me insane. They wanted me, needed me. If he had been an actual threat, they'd have warned me, protected me against harm. Instead, he stopped just short, and I adjusted my gaze to stare him in the face.

"Can you hear me?"

The orderly oozed aggression, a cheap perfume of chaos that wafted off him. When I turned, my eyes staring into his, the bravado faded. They were used to operating freely, the diseases infecting our brains rendering them invisible. No animosity, no anger, just simple eye contact and I rendered the man inert. It took a moment before the ghosts returned, showing his head turned from our tawdry love affair.

His ghost spoke with another, a man in a lab coat. I recognized the doctor whose stern face and extended finger gave away his displeasure. Seconds later, the man caught up to his ghost, the two joining until his spindly pointer finger jabbed the orderly in the chest. I had only been here for a few days and already I knew the man in the coat ruled with an iron fist. It was time for me to join his faithful subjects.

"Eleanor Bouvier," he said. "Is that your name?"

"Yes, doctor," the orderly said. "She's mute, hasn't spoken since her mother dropped her off."

"Oh, alright," the doctor eyed a clipboard with a stack of papers attached to the top. "Your previous doctor says you've been mute for…" He thumbed through the papers. Since Poppa died, Momma started working as a nurse. It began well enough, but when Benjie died, the drinking started and a series of men came and went in our house. Broken and unable to piece herself back together, she left me here, hoping they could do a better job. I wanted to be angry, to lash out, but there was no point in demanding she take me back. The ghosts had revealed my future months before it happened. Now I only ran through the motions.

"Your brother died. You've been mute since?" I hardly moved my eyes as he scribbled on a sheet of paper. "It says you watched it happen but didn't try to help him? What kind of person can watch their sibling die?"

The doctor wasn't seeking an answer. His ghost had already turned to the orderly, and they talked. For a moment, I could imagine they spoke about a way to fix me, to make the devils invisible once more. But the curse bestowed upon me had yet to reach its conclusion.

"She's most likely mute due to early-onset psychosis. You know the dosages. Make sure she takes them all. I don't need another one of the patients getting attacked."

They both walked away, and I continued staring out the window. I imagined the cool sensation of it pressed against my cheek. The moisture between the glass and my skin would gather until it dripped. Inhaling, I'd only be able to smell the fresh air attempting to force its way inside this less-than-sterile environment. All that would stand between me and freedom, a quarter inch of glass. With a hard enough knock from my knuckles, I could be free.

But not from them.

The ghosts haunted me no matter where I went. If I made it out the window and fled the hospital, I'd be alone and freezing. On my deathbed, drawing in shallow breaths, willing myself to die, the ghosts would appear. Clawing at me, they'd drag me into the earth while death opened the door to Hell. No, I'd never be free. This was my burden, my cross to bear.

"Welcome to Riverview Manor," the orderly said as he walked into view. He held his fist shut, and I knew from watching, it would hold my medications. I had no idea what they might do, but I prayed that they helped me get better. If I couldn't save myself, I'd rely on the hospital to help.

"I'm going to put these pills in your mouth. If you bite me, we'll send you to confinement. Do you understand?" He waited an appropriate amount of time before pinching the sides of my jaw. My mouth opened without resistance and he shoveled in five or six pills. I was about to swallow them when he held a cup of water to my lips. A few sips later and he stepped back, admiring his handiwork.

I thought he'd leave, but instead he grabbed a chair from a nearby table and sat across from me, obscuring my view out the windows. He sat down and rested his forearms on his thighs while he studied my face. He might have been considered hand-some except for the dingy mustache desperately clinging to the top of his lip.

"I beat my mother," he confessed. "I know, I know. We're not supposed to talk about personal matters with patients, but I trust you, Eleanor. I feel like we have a genuine connection."

My punishment persisted. Not only did the ghosts continue to step in and out of the people about the room, but the orderly insisted I serve as his spiritual guide.

"I've been stealing medicine. It's not for me, I wouldn't touch that stuff. But people pay good money for it." He rested a hand on my knee. I didn't look down to see. "If the medicine doesn't help, they'll be forced to drill inside that noggin of yours." He made a cranking motion and then illustrated the splatter to be more disgusting. "Then they'll release the demons running around in your head."

Release the demons, I could only hope.

"Best hope those meds help, dear. I would hate to see a dame as pretty as yourself need the operation." He leaned forward, brushing a piece of hair behind my ear. "I think this is the start of a beautiful friendship." He stood, patted me on the head like a child, and then left.

The ghosts weren't the most despicable devils in this hospital.

Chapter Nine

1942

"Eleanor, I can't believe you're being so reckless."

Sitting opposite Frank's cluttered desk, I slinked down in the chair. I gave him every detail, from the mask to the charcoal to the three dead men. The frown grew more serious as I revealed my warning for delivery to Bertolucci.

"What if the man from yesterday recognized you?"

"He's dead."

"That doesn't make it better." He shook his head. "No, in fact, that makes this even worse. Eleanor, you can't go around killing anybody who gets in your way."

Frank proved himself to be a more than capable father. He reluctantly assumed the mantle as a bit of wayward camaraderie with my birth father. But over the years he had grown into the role. I commended him for taking responsibility for a young girl he had no connection with.

"This isn't killing for fun."

"I'm not sure that makes it better."

"If he had come back and threatened the gym? What if he threatened Susan Lee while she worked? What if…"

"You can't live in a world of what-ifs, Eleanor."

More than any other person alive, Frank understood my temporal displacement. I lived half in the present and half in the future. I knew of a changed world that would descend upon us in the next few decades. It came with the rise of women's liberation and the acceptance of racial differences. I knew there was a world emerging, unlike anything humans understood. *Despite my* knowing, everybody else remained oblivious.

"Frank," I said calmly, straightening my back, "I live in a world without what-ifs. I know the future. I know what's coming."

"And?"

"Change is in the air. Susan Lee is ensuring the success of our troops. You're saving the broken men out there. What am I doing?"

"You do plenty."

I adored Frank. Despite our rocky beginnings, the man had a heart of gold. Together we had weathered more than one storm. But he still only saw me as a young woman. He had difficulty reconciling that I was unlike any other human.

"I can do more," I said with a flat tone. "This is my city, Frank. And I'll be damned if somebody is going to try and wrestle it out from underneath our feet."

He sat back in his chair. His expression moved from concern to defeat. It had to be difficult arguing with a girl who knew the outcome of every discussion. If I had summoned the ghosts, I could have avoided the majority of this conversation and jumped to the finale. Frank hated when I ended our discussions before they started. We did not have typical father/daughter problems.

"You're going to do it anyway."

"I am." Honesty remained the bedrock of our relationship.

"I'm going to go out with you. You can't do this alone."

He would. I don't know if I could convince him to wear a mask. It could be interesting having a sidekick, somebody to watch my back. But if I wouldn't allow Edward to join me, even with his abilities able to turn the tide, I wouldn't let Frank.

"This is my journey."

"You're doing it alone?"

I nodded. "You have a purpose. You came back from rock bottom. Now you're providing a bastion for those in need. You're giving these men back their lives. You're helping drunks turn their lives around. Frank, if anything, I'm doing this because of you."

I swore his cheeks turned a shade of red. There was no plan to stroke his ego. I hadn't given it much thought up to this point. But he was indeed an inspiration. I could stop being a grouchy woman long enough to admit it.

"Thanks, 'Nore, but I'll still be going out with you."

I didn't like it, but I finally relented. "Fine."

"I expected you to put up more of a fight."

"I would have, but I'm not making any progress on this Society. So I might as well focus on something I can change. Who knows, perhaps you'll have some insight."

Frank's eyes lit up. Mentioning the Society had him leaning forward and rummaging around on his desk. Like Edward, I requested Frank ask his fighters for any word on the organization. We had nothing but a name and a symbol for leads. Up to this point, everybody raised an eyebrow, unsure why we were asking.

"Last night at support," he pushed a book to the side, "we had a few new members. We're going to need to start having a third group night. It seems word has gotten out."

More than once I'd found Frank unconscious at the bar, passed out with his head lying in a sticky puddle of stale beer. Harry had grown accustomed to phoning me in the evening to retrieve the man. I understood the agony that drove him to drink. I refused to summon the ghosts to see his future, fearful they'd reveal the moment he drank himself to death. Ultimately,

I gave him a choice, be the father I needed or we say our farewells.

Four months passed. Sitting in the apartment, reading with Susan Lee, the phone rang. She called me to the phone, and on the other end, I heard sobbing. Frank had reached rock bottom. He begged for forgiveness and while I prepared to end the phone call in an act of tough love, he said the magic phrase. "I need help."

He snatched up a sheet of paper.

I tried to push the image of the crying man from my mind. Our relationship endured. Never touching another drop of whiskey, he climbed his way up from the hole. But it wasn't enough to persevere. Now, he shared his story with others, holding meetings for those with similar stories.

"Three wavy lines, right?"

I pushed away the memory as Frank showed me the sheet of paper. The sigil was identical to the symbol I had seen in the doctor's study. My mind raced. Where had Frank come about the symbol? Had the Society come to New York?

"Did somebody recognize it?"

Frank shook his head. "I'm violating the whole point of Alcoholics Anonymous," he handed me the sheet. The scribbles weren't perfect, but it was an obvious match. "One of the new men at the meeting had that tattooed on the underside of his right wrist."

A clue.

"Eleanor," Frank placed his hand on mine. "Don't hurt him. He's struggling."

I didn't know what to say. If he was part of an organization trying to eradicate mentalists, there were no promises. Was he destined to be one of those mindless killers, or was he a mentalist himself?

"I can't make any promises."

The same stern look as before. He violated one of the most

important tenants of Alcoholics Anonymous to give me the information. I gave him a low moan.

"I'll try not to."

"It's all I can ask."

I stared at the sheet of paper, recalling the book in the doctor's study. It was the first clue that there were more of this Society in the city. I tried not to speculate, tried not to imagine where it would take me. I wondered if I could leverage the information with Gregory and convince him to explain how he knew they were here. Tomorrow when I meet with him, I'd press him until he finally spoke.

"If you don't get out there, Koji is going to think you're ignoring him."

The bruise on my chest had all but faded, but I remembered the ache. After yesterday's scuffle, I knew I needed the session. If I was going to rid the city of this growing plague, I would have to train harder, longer.

Today, I pieced together an abstract puzzle.

Chapter Ten

1942

I couldn't imagine living anywhere other than New York. The memories of the Midwest had become blurry and difficult to muster. I often thought about returning to the farm to see if it survived. Each time the idea surfaced, I buried it beneath a list of excuses.

I walked along the street, oblivious to the gentleman walking toward me. I bumped into him, lost in thought. Like a true New Yorker, he shot me a dirty look and continued walking. I mumbled an apology he couldn't possibly hear. Despite being in one of the largest cities in the United States, we were each left with a sense of isolation.

To my right, Central Park sprawled across the center of the city. Amidst a jungle of stone and steel, this lush escape persisted. During the day, the park offered trails and a lovely lake. One could spend hours walking idly about, never reaching the other side. It offered a change of pace in an otherwise fast-moving city. As long as the sun hung high in the sky, the park offered refuge.

I reached into my pocket and pulled out two crumpled pieces

of paper. One held the drawing of the wavy lines, the other held an address. I needed to connect my vision of the future with my now. Normally I couldn't place a location or a time. For once, it was different. I could at least stand before the church and feel a connection to the otherworldliness of my abilities.

I gave a slight laugh as I realized I was looking at the address as a tall steeple punched its way above other nearby buildings. Shoving the paper into my pocket, I continued walking. The sidewalk continued going on for eternity, but I stopped when the wrought-iron fence started. Behind the gates, the church held a small yard. In the middle, a cross stood almost four feet tall, as one might expect.

Churches were plenty in New York, but this one appeared more modest than the atrocities that begged for attention. It was larger than my apartment building, or even the gym. I imagined that each stone had been placed by a person needing a place to worship. I let my fingers run along the fence, and I swore I could feel the hum of energy in each pole.

The ghosts flooded the street. For the first time in months, they demanded to be seen. Hundreds if not thousands of ghosts moved about, entering the double gates, flooding into the church. I often scoffed at those who found the need to believe in a higher power, spoiled acolytes believing God singled them out for greatness.

These were not them. The men, women, and children ushered along to the church were the wretches of New York City. Patchwork clothes and modest means moved in a line to reach the service. I stood in the middle of the flood and pondered what made this church special? I would have left with the question unanswered until I saw my own ghost step forward and disappear amongst the droves.

"It wouldn't hurt," I said as I put my hand on the fence. "I can tolerate the zealots for a while."

No lock or chain prevented me from entering. The fence stood as a warning, but those inside felt no need to prevent men and women from entering. Its courtyard was well maintained, and the shrubs had recently been clipped. The large red door stood as a testament to a long-forgotten time. The wood was battered and bruised from frequent knocking and the large hinges appeared rusty but well used. For a moment, I contemplated if I should use the door knocker or let myself in.

I reached out, letting my fingers run over the iron circle used to signal guests. The door opened, and I pulled my hand back, almost jumping away from the door. For a moment, I considered turning and running. Funny thing, bravery, I had no problem with a man pointing a gun at my head, but a nun, she frightened me.

"Hello there," said a soft voice. I expected it to be the woman from my vision. I studied the eyes, and I had to admit, I felt a sense of sadness when I realized it wasn't her.

"Uhh." How does one greet a nun?

"Please do come in. I was just about to go for a walk. I didn't mean to startle you."

"My apologies…" I raised an eyebrow, forcing the confusion onto my face.

"Sister," she said with a smile. "Sister Beatrice."

"Sister Beatrice, I'm sorry. I was walking by and something… I can't quite explain it."

Sister Beatrice laughed, her voice cheery and the lines around her lips well worn. I expected a nun to be solemn, quiet. Sister Beatrice's demeanor melted away my apprehension, and I found myself disarmed. She stepped back, opening the door wider, inviting me in.

"Welcome to St. Morgan's Church."

"Thank you, Sister." Once inside, I found New York City absent. The towering buildings filled with steel and glass vanished in a structure built of stone. It held so much history that

I couldn't help but feel a moment of belief. Hairs along my arms stood on end and I took a moment to collect myself.

"It's beautiful," I said.

Sister Beatrice shut the door and walked with me through the lobby. I had expected the crosses, the painting of Mary holding her son, Jesus. I might not partake in religion, but growing up on a farm in the Midwest, they forced us to endure Sunday school. My house had never been particularly religious, but we'd said our bedtime prayers when I was young.

"What brings you here today?"

"Is it wrong that I have no idea?"

"God has summoned us here for many reasons. It might not be clear now, but he has his way of speaking to us."

"I've never been particularly devout."

I don't know why I admitted that. Standing here in this holiest of places, it felt improper to lie. I found that more often than not, the truth is more uncanny than any lie I could muster.

"That's alright," she said stepping up to the table that held a collection of candles. There were nearly a hundred unlit wicks. She offered me a match. "Strike the match and light the candle. We offer the flame to the Almighty." I did as instructed, striking the match and lighting a votive.

"We each take a journey to find our faith. Don't feel as if there is any right or wrong way."

"You sound much different from the nuns at Sunday school."

"The Sisters and I find it is best to help those who need it most. Our way is not the only way. We know this. Others might call it blasphemy. I like to think in a time of strife, we are the warriors willing to defend those who cannot defend themselves."

For a moment, I wondered if the nun knew more than she was letting on. Did some divine voice unmask me? There was an urge to run, to bolt for the door before she uncovered any more of my secrets.

"I have a feeling you understand my words more than most."

I needed to change the topic before I fled. "Do you take in orphans?"

The question had her staring at my belly. I shook my head. "No, not for me. I just—"

"You're an orphan?"

I hadn't given it much thought, but the moment my mother left me at the hospital, I guess I had become one. I clung to the image of Frank, him breaking into the room and rescuing me from death. The man had become my father, stolen me from a world of isolation, and given me a new definition of family.

"I was," I smiled. "My mother gave me up when I was too old for an orphanage but too young to survive on my own."

"I'm sorry to hear this."

I believed her. Sister Beatrice felt the sadness of my words, her eyelids growing heavy and her lips tense with concern. "It ends well though. Not a happy ending, but a satisfactory one. A man who owed me nothing took me in and gives me unconditional love."

Sister Beatrice didn't ask permission as she wrapped her arms about my torso. She squeezed, an expert in the art of hugging. I returned the sentiment. Perhaps if she had been the nun reading to me during Sunday school, I might have found more comfort in religion. Minutes ago, we had been strangers, but I already felt as if she cared for me like one of her own.

"This brings me joy. We have many young girls here. We have fought tooth and nail to make sure the orphanage remains open. These girls have nobody, so we do what we can for them before they enter the world."

"Girls? Not infants or babies?"

"Oh no," she said, stepping back from me. "We are but tired old women. We struggle with the youngest girls, but none of us has the experience or expertise to raise an infant."

For a moment, I feared my vision might be wrong, or that I might have glimpsed into a future far from the now. I had no way of knowing. Despite being out of step with the timeline, I had to smile. It was the first time I witnessed the future and had the luxury of experiencing the place. If this was as close as I could get, it was enough.

"Please go in and sit. I'm sure a moment with the Lord would do your soul some good. It has been a quiet day, so you have the church to yourself."

She guided me toward one of the doors further into the nave. The stonework continued and beautifully carved pews lined either side of the aisle. I might not be religious, but I could feel an awe-inspiring sensation spread along my skin. The light poured through stain glass windows and I could imagine the seats filled with parishioners recommitting themselves to the divine. Is this what Gregory felt when he touched another person's emotions?

"Thank you, Sister Beatrice."

"Thank me not, it is the Lord that tempted me to open the door at that very moment." She stood at the entrance as I walked down the aisle. "God bless," she mumbled before vanishing.

I took a knee as I approached the altar. Making the sign of the cross, I found it difficult to do away with a decade of reciting the Lord's Prayer. I might not believe, but I found a bit of comfort in the ritual of worship. Taking a spot in a pew to the left, I had a front-row seat to the splendors of the church.

A massive cross sat in the back of the altar, Jesus suspended from the nails driven into his hands and feet. There were fresh flowers lining the steps up onto the altar, recently replaced by the church's caretaker. The Sisters cared for this house, putting forth the best the church offered.

I had no words to exchange with a vacant God. To whisper a prayer, I felt I'd be betraying myself, giving in to peer pressure. I might not believe in this higher power, but I still respected those who found comfort in faith. I rested my hands in my lap, admiring the intricate depictions of the disciples in the stained-glass windows. The iconography of Christ assaulted me at every turn.

Ghosts snapped into existence. Twice since coming here, they found it important to make themselves known. I'd have to discuss this with Gregory when I saw him next. Since I learned to summon them, they hadn't felt the need to violate my space unless requested. I almost chuckled, thinking that perhaps God was working through the phantoms of the future.

The priest stood at the pulpit, reading from the Bible to his flock. Men and women kneeled, hands clasped together as they beseeched their savior. Rows of parishioners stood in line, waiting to take the sacrament before the end of the service. Nothing struck me as out of sorts. Looking for a clue from the ghosts, I turned about in my seat.

"Hi."

I jumped. Behind me, a young girl with pigtails smiled. One of her adult teeth had yet to grow into place. Her face beamed with excitement, oblivious of her unsettling presence.

"Hi," I said, confused.

I studied the young girl's face. She couldn't have reached her tenth birthday. Her hair pulled back made it difficult for me to sort out how old she might be. However, the white blouse and black skirt gave away she was a student at one of the many Catholic schools in this part of the city.

"Sister Beatrice wanted me to say hello."

"Did she now?" I pivoted in my seat, getting comfortable. I forced the invisible flame away, and the ghosts vanished, and only the girl and I remained in the church.

"My name is Dorothy. What's your name?"

"Eleanor," I said. She held out her hand, prepared to shake. I extended my hand. She gave it a vigorous up and down.

"That's a pretty name."

I blushed. I assumed she was an orphan of the church. Had Sister Beatrice sent her to talk to me about being an orphan? I could beat up a mugger without batting an eye, but a child made me uneasy. Motherhood would never be in my future, and I started to understand why.

"Dorothy is a pretty name too."

She dropped her chin, bashful at the compliment. "Sister Beatrice gave me that name. She said it means that I'm a gift from God."

"I see." I smiled, connecting the name to my past. "Do you know any other Dorothy's?" The girl shook her head. "Dorothy is a character in my favorite novel growing up. Have you read *The Wonderful Wizard of Oz*?"

The girl scooted to the edge of her pew, excited to hear about a girl sharing her name. "Did she have pigtails?"

"She did!" Her eyes grew wide. "There was a scary tornado, and she found herself in a magical land. She was a brave little girl, just like you."

"Really?"

"An evil witch tried to stop her from rescuing her friends. She met a scarecrow, a tin man, and a cowardly lion. But she beat the witch. She saved all of Oz. Then she managed to find her way home."

"Wow."

"I bet you're brave just like her."

"Sister Beatrice says you're an orphan like me."

I nodded. "When I was young, my dad died, and my mom couldn't take care of me anymore. She loved me very much, but she couldn't keep me."

"Sister Beatrice says my mom loved me and that's why she brought me to the church."

"I'm sure she did." Grappling with the reality that Momma had given me up had been tough. I resented her, hated even. After Benjie died, she lost the light in her eyes. She couldn't tolerate my refusal to speak. One morning over breakfast, she broke, and we took a trip to the hospital. It was the last time I ever saw the woman.

"How do you like living here?"

"We don't live here silly, this is a church." The girl's laughter forced a grin on my face. Despite the hardships of the world, she giggled her way through the day. "We live next door in the orphanage. It's nice. There are lots of other girls to play with. Maggie braided my hair this morning."

"Well, you tell Maggie she did a wonderful job."

"I will," she said, standing up. "I have to get back to school. Sister Beatrice told me to not stay too long."

"It sounds like Sister Beatrice is making sure you're really smart when you grow up. You'll be able to do anything you want."

"I'm going to be a nun," the girl said. "I want to be just like Sister Beatrice."

The hair on the back of my neck stood on end as I put together the pieces. I looked up to the cross suspended in the air and found a wooden Jesus. I swore his lips were turned up in a smile.

"Dorothy, what's your last name?"

She stood in the aisle, already making her way from the church. The young girl turned around and gave me a curtsey. "Dorothy Muriel," she said without missing a beat. The girl skipped between the pews until she exited.

For the first time, I not only found the location of a vision, but I found myself part of a bigger picture. Decades early, I met the nun holding a baby child, and it made sense. Refusing to give up the infant, I understood her desire to raise the baby herself. I had no idea why the vision mattered, but I suddenly felt I was part of a bigger story I had yet to unravel.

"Sister Muriel," I whispered. My heart swelled at the thought of the young girl growing into the keeper of this sacred space.

Tears formed in the corner of my eyes and I wiped them clear.

I don't believe I found myself any closer to the deity watching over this building. There was little to no chance I would ever believe in God again. However, I did find a glimmer of faith in myself.

"Thank you, God."

Chapter Eleven

1942

The ladies of the night had no desire to hide. They were loud and shouted back and forth to one another. I couldn't fathom what brought them to this line of work, or how they continued coming out night after night. But word on the street said they were in trouble. The same men shaking down storefronts were abusing the women who received payment to accompany men to their hotel rooms.

I loathed men abusing women.

I sat across the street, watching the brightly colored women whistle and call every man who walked by. Some men held their heads down, staring at their feet as they passed. However, more often than not, men gawked, admiring the women who dared show more skin than typically acceptable. I didn't understand them, but I admired the freedom with which they moved. They were fearless. We might have different purposes tonight, but we wouldn't let the crime scouring the streets of New York stop us from venturing out.

They gathered on the corner. The building behind them, a hotel with a large bar on the first floor. They waited for a patron to step outside and choose a lady before retreating to their room for a night of carnal pleasure. I hid amongst the shadows in an alley across the street, giving me the perfect vantage point for any disturbances.

As the night wore on, gentlemen stepped outside, talking with the women. I had never given it much thought, but it was no different from any other transaction. You shopped for what you craved, haggled the price, paid, and went about your business to enjoy your purchase. I found the entire ordeal fascinating, their ability to use their bodies for income.

Two men in brown trench coats approached. I stepped further into the shadow when they flashed their badges. I expected the women to disperse at the sight of law enforcement, but instead, they huddled together. The women closed ranks, protecting the youngest girls. I had a newfound respect for these women. While I didn't expect a run-in with the law, I'd risk the encounter to protect them.

A woman reluctantly stepped forward, the other women holding her hand until she pulled away. Her fair skin and dark hair made her striking. Her deep red dress left little to the imagination, a plunging neckline and snug fit revealed her curves. The two policemen followed her into the hotel.

I crossed the street, keeping my face low as I went. I paused for a moment, listening to the rapid conversation by the ladies.

"You go in and ask them to stop."

"Remember Paula?" The woman's face scrunched up in distaste.

"I haven't seen her, since."

"Stay away, girl, they're trouble."

I breezed by them and into the lobby. To my right, a bar was filled with gentlemen smoking and partaking in glasses of scotch. Already, the two gentlemen and their victim had vanished. I was in no rush. I need to give the gentlemen a moment to get comfortable before I stormed through the hotel door.

"The two officers," I snapped my fingers at the man behind the desk. "What room are they in?"

He gave me a slight glance before returning to distributing the mail. I had no patience for misogyny. "You're supplying them a room. If I find out this is true, I will tear your testicles from your body."

"Ma'am," he gave a slight laugh. "Perhaps you've had one too many—"

I reached over the counter, grabbing him by the back of the neck. I pulled his head onto the desk, reaching for the metal spike where they stacked messages for patrons. I rested it against his cheek. "Them, or you."

"One-thirteen, down the hall, take a right, last door on the left."

"You're going to want to call the cops in a few minutes."

"Who the hell are you?"

I had no desire to answer. I stormed down the hallway, pulling my hair back and lifting the mask. I had a moment to consider the fight. The room would be small, tight with four people. This would be about precision, blocking, and dodging. I couldn't rely on theatrics. The men's sheer size put them at an advantage.

"I can do this," I whispered. "I must do this. The city needs me."

My fingers ground against the charcoal, coating my fingers. With a swipe across my eyes I was ready. The flame stood at attention, ready to be manipulated. The hallway mirror to my right revealed a fierce woman. I didn't want to admit it, or at least not say it aloud, but I had discovered my pride. I stood straight as the ghost stepped from my body, invisible in the mirror's reflection.

It let me see through the door. A woman cried on the bed. The taller, older officer unbuttoned his pants, but the shorter, chubbier man opted to drop his trousers before removing his shirt. The scene nearly made me wretch, the sight of men inflicting such terror on a woman. My ghost vanished, and I stood in the hallway, squaring myself a few feet from the door. It would end tonight.

Raising my heel, I slammed it against the door, just north of the handle. It flung open, smacking the man with his pants around his ankles. The disbelief, the complete and utter refusal to believe somebody, especially a woman, would dare to defy them left me smiling. I could have basked in his realization, but he reached for his jacket.

"No." The statement erupted from confidence. I walked into the room and the ghosts of the three moved just out of time with their bodies. The world slowed, and the man lunged for his gun while the man behind the door toppled onto the bed. The woman hardly moved, her ghost curling up in a ball. Tight, precise, and swift movements went through my head. I didn't have time to taunt my prey.

I kicked the door wider while leaning forward, grabbing the tall man's jacket. The door slammed into his companion while I pulled his jacket out of reach. The gun thumped on the floor. He tried to slam a fist against the side of my head. I ducked below the pathetic attempt. I jabbed at his groin. He backed away, so I grazed his trousers, enough to ward him away, but not enough to cause damage.

To my right, a dresser and a well-used armchair held the men's discarded clothing. The bed took up the majority of the space, the girl huddled by the headboard while the chubby officer crawled over the bed, eager to join the fray.

The tall man leaned into the right hook. I stepped back, using the back of my right hand to guide it, crossing his body to prevent him from following with a left. I'd thank Koji later for the tactic. Turning, I brought my fist down on the chubby man's face just as he reached the foot of the bed. The heel of my right foot lifted, drilling into the tall man's knee.

Proximity worked in my favor, offering them a false sense of security. Law enforcement believed they were the apex predators. I shattered the tall man's belief—and his knee cap. The man on the bed had more stamina, shaking off my punch as if it were nothing. He got onto his knees on the bed, to capture me in a bearhug.

"No," I repeated.

I stepped uncomfortably close to the tall man, out of reach of the chubby officer. The tall man hadn't finished howling from the broken knee when I slammed my forehead into his face, striking his nose with a loud crack. Had he been younger, perhaps less concerned for his own well-being, he might have thought to grab me. Instead, he grabbed his nose, catching a wave of blood dripping from the tip.

I held his open shirt, using it for leverage as I bent low at the waist, kicking the chubby man in the torso. He toppled backward, rolling off the bed in the space between it and the wall. I swung my knee back, standing upright, slamming it into the groin of the tall man. Now, as he screamed at the top of his lungs, I found myself smiling.

"Look out," yelled the girl.

I summoned the ghosts. The world slowed, giving me an opportunity to examine my options. The ghost of the man held his gun upright, partially holstered as he fumbled for the trigger. I only had a moment to react before he shook it free and fired. The man had no qualm striking his companion. Loyalty vanished when it came to saving his own skin.

The ghosts vanished, and I somersaulted onto the bed. With the heel of my right boot stretched out, I slid into the man, striking him along the collarbone. He tried to point the weapon, but I used my left foot to pin his arm to the wall. With a stomp, I forced the weapon from his hand. I gripped the sheets, trying to give myself leverage as I swiped my right foot across his face.

The man's body went limp, propped up by the wall. I slid off the bed, retrieving the pistol, emptying the bullets onto the floor before tossing it on the other side of the bed. The tall man had fallen to his knees, bloody hands cupping his manhood. I found myself more than satisfied with the outcome. The two men would wake up in the morning, embarrassed, and in pain. They'd remember this moment when they considered cornering another call girl.

"Are you okay?"

The girl's eyes were wide, terrified of me almost as much as them. At least with the officers, she knew what was about to happen. Right now, she wasn't sure if I was a savior or another person about to take out their aggressions.

"Are you okay?" I repeated the question firmly.

She nodded.

Reaching into my pocket, I slid my fingers into the brass knuckles. I spun about on the bed, getting to my feet in front of the tall man. I noticed the graying hair at his temples. What childhood trauma had led him to these decisions? I pushed the question aside. Truthfully, I didn't care.

I reached back. One solid blow to the side of his head and the man collapsed. The image in the mirror on the dresser was horrific. Blood had splattered across my face, spray from breaking his nose. Smeared and red, I wore it as a badge, a compliment on a job well done.

"You should leave."

"Wha—What are you going to do?"

"They deserved a lesson in humility. Tell the other women I'm doing what I can. If they come again, I will be sure to deal with them. Permanently." I just threatened to kill two of New York City's police officers. Even for me, that seemed to reach far over the line I tried to maintain.

She nodded her head. Sliding off the bed, she stepped into the hallway. I didn't need to be an empath to see she was as terrified of me as them. Once she told the other girls, my reputation would spread. It'd only be a matter of time before the whispers of a crazed woman reached Bertolucci. Good.

It took some time, but I liberated the gentlemen of their clothes. Opening the window, I dumped them into the street. I wanted them to wake, confused over what had transpired. I chucked their guns down the alley and then exited, walking down the hallway, back straight and confident.

When I reached the front desk, the man paused, terrified of the gory mess splattered across my eyes and forehead. "If I hear you're helping them take advantage of these women again. I'll kill you."

There was no need for a response. I exited.

"Oh my," one woman howled.

"Thank you," cheered others.

I walked through the crowd of call girls. Eyes forward, I gave them a slight nod as I vanished into the alley. A vengeful woman, a vigilante, watched over those ignored by the city. One act at a time, I reclaimed my home.

Chapter Twelve

1931

At first I prayed the treatments would rid me of the demons. The ghosts had become relentless, stalking me whether I was awake or asleep. According to the doctors, I was not well. When Momma let the men take me away, I tried to resist. But they were right. I was sick. The ghosts ushered me further from sanity.

"Eleanor," his voice was more nasally than normal. I should be freezing. The ice in the bath had nearly melted. On a cool day, it took almost three hours. It must be closer to four since the nurses had helped me out of my robe and placed me in the ice-filled tub.

Speaking wasn't an option. My jaw hurt from the chattering. I gripped my legs, pulling my knees tightly to my chest. Both of my hands hurt from being submerged for so long, but as I ran them along my skin, I couldn't feel my fingers or my thighs. The ghosts were nowhere to be found. Between the initial plunge below the surface of the water and the numbness, the specters dissipated.

"Eleanor," he snapped. Dr. Gustofson often reminded me that

his time was valuable and there were more grateful patients waiting for his attention. I did not like him, nor did I care for his tone. The first few weeks I lunged at him. He demanded the orderlies to bind my arms in the stiff fabric of a white coat. I no longer responded, but I refused to acknowledge him when he spoke my name.

"Another hour might be in order."

Fearful, I turned my head. I expected to see the slight rise of his lip giving away his smug satisfaction. Either the doctor believed he had corrected the broken parts of my mind, or he was a masochist. I suspected he took pleasure in breaking me further.

The ghosts had returned.

The doctor stood transparent, examining a clipboard. I could see through him to the white door leading into the room. The ghost spoke my name again. Splitting into two, his ghost kneeled at the foot of the tub, staring me in the face. The translucent twin knelt next to me, glaring down his long slender nose.

"No." I manage the single word through clamped teeth, but it was pointless. The ghosts never listen. The man at the foot of the tub reached into the water and gave me a phantom splash. I clenched my eyes tightly, trying to will away the taunting demons. I keep hoping that the Lord would grant me mercy and when I open them, they'll have vanished.

"Eleanor." It's him, the real him.

Through slivers, I saw Dr. Gustofson standing just inside the room. He flipped through the pages of his clipboard. He's solid and I couldn't see through him to the door on the other side. Tilting his head curiously to the side, he took his time as he inspected me. Two steps closer and he's stood at my side, next to the tub.

"Eleanor, are you seeing them now?"

My muscles tightened to where a slight shake of my head made me wince in pain. The scribbling of his pen on the paper was the only sound. The longer it took him to write his thoughts, the worse the diagnosis. Three strong swipes of the pen meant he's emphasized something. I wondered if the doctor was allowed to use words like "crazy" or "demented" or if only the orderlies called me that.

Now, the ghosts hid when there was another person in the room. I wondered if the transparent hauntings waited until I was alone to send me into hysterics. They either came when I was minding my own business or when bad things happened.

The ghosts liked bad things.

The specter of a nurse burst into the room. It's a silent affair. The door didn't make a sound as it opened, nor could I hear her panting as her eyes emoted sheer terror. The woman's white blouse was covered in red and with a darkening line of blood on her forearm. A ghost stepped out of the doctor's opaque form. He threw the clipboard across the room and held the nurse by the shoulders, violently shaking her. I couldn't hear the words, but whatever she said had him worried as well.

"But now you are?" asked the actual doctor. He followed my line of sight, staring at the door where my eyes remained fixated.

"Do these ghosts tell you to do things?"

I gave him a slight shake of the head, careful not to hurt my neck. He scribbled again. His ghostly version was busy helping the nurse to the floor. She put pressure on her arm while he stepped up to the door. Peeking out, he looked back and forth, and like that he left. Something bad was going to happen, that's how it always went. The nurse on the floor was still in hysterics as she stared at me. Just as I saw through her, she seemed to stare through me.

"When do you see them most, Eleanor?"

"When..." I couldn't unclench my teeth to speak normally. "Bad things..." It almost hurt. "Happen..."

This time when the door opened, it was accompanied by sound. I preferred the nurse's whimpering to her silent twin. Just like the ghosts, he helped her to the floor, and with a quick glance, he was out the door.

There was screaming coming from outside, louder than normal and far more chaotic. Many nights I woke from sleep to the sounds of a patient howling at the moon or shouting. There was something different between the screams of a crazy and a sane person. Sane people yelled out in reaction, whereas those residing at the hospital did it to cause a reaction. Outside the door, sane people cried out.

There was a commotion. Shouting. I tried to make out the individual words, but I could only hear garbled voices. One of them belonged to Dr. Gustofson. There was a bark and then a thump against the wall. The panicked talking retreated into the asylum. It took the nurse the better part of five minutes before she caught her breath, enough to compose herself.

One of the patients burst into the room. Isaac's face held a mix of anger and confusion. Crimson lines crisscrossed down his gown. Here, it was commonplace for a patient to have blood on them. Between the arm scratching, bloody noses, or bitten lips, most patients went to bed at night with at least one or two blotchy bloodstains. His though, they were more of a splattering, a deep dark color that only came from a wound more serious than a cut.

Time froze. The ghosts returned with a vengeance.

Isaac's ghost lunged for the nurse, wrestling with her own specter. He pinned her to the floor. I caught the glimmer of a scalpel. With a single slash, he severed something in her neck that left her limp. I'm not shocked, not in this place.

Something was wrong. Normally I experienced multiple ghosts of a person showing the linear progression of time. Each represented events tied together but separated by seconds. But there were two additional ghosts of Isaac, unconnected.

His second ghost cowered in the corner, hiding from the orderlies. The other specter walked to the other side of my tub.

His arm wrapped around my neck. He waited for the door. He planned on using me to ward away whoever came into the room. The door flew open and in his paranoia, I could feel the phantom blade press into my neck. I gasped at the sensation, thankful to finally put this never-ending nightmare behind me.

I wanted to tempt him, to hurl an insult or scream.

A third ghost was knocked forward as see-through orderlies burst through the door. They were on him, bending his arm in a way that would surely break his elbow. I had a twenty-five percent chance that he'd free me. One future out of four meant an end of demons showing me things I never asked to see.

My lips trembled. "Me."

A single word forced the ghosts to retreat, leaving me, the nurse, and Isaac alone. His eyes focused on me. They flashed to her before settling on my tiny form shivering in the tub. He took a step in my direction before the door flew open, hurling the man to the ground. Two men in uniform leaped onto Isaac, grabbing for the hand gripping the scalpel. There was a crunching sound as his elbow snapped in half. He howled loud enough that I flinched.

It's over. They dragged a whining Isaac from the room. The nurse only returned to looking at me when I sobbed. She continued applying pressure to the cut on her arm as she walked on her knees closer to me.

"You're safe now," she said as she pulled me to the side of the tub so she could cradle my head. "He's gone. You'll be safe, child."

Sobbing turned to crying. She squeezed my face against her bosom. Doctors had tried medicine and now they attempted to excise the demons in a bath of frozen water. The options dwindled and it wouldn't be long before they resorted to something drastic. I didn't want them to drill into my skull. But I wanted to finally be free.

Isaac could have stopped the demons and silenced the ghosts

once and for all. I should have yelled or begged. It could have been different this time. A single word made him take a step in my direction. Maybe it meant I could change the future? If I had been stronger, perhaps I could have willed him to me, and with a slow drag of the blade, it would be over.

I was alive. I wasn't strong enough to die.

Chapter Thirteen

1942

"Who are they?" The words came out with more of a growl than I intended.

Despite the sun shining and lazy clouds drifting across the sky, my disposition was more than sour. I didn't care about the chirping birds or squirrels chasing one another in an attempt to snag a fallen acorn. I didn't find any use in beating around the bush with a man who could read my emotions.

"The Society, Gregory. What do you know? Tell me."

"I'm not sure you want to know."

Straightening my back, I flattened out the front of my slacks. I rested one hand on top of the other in my lap. With ankles crossed, I appeared to be the perfect lady. However, beneath the surface, a seething rage built. Gregory knew far more than he had offered, and with evidence of the Society lurking in the city, I had no time to play his games. I allowed the anger to sit in the pit of my stomach, a ball of red light. I pushed it forward, imagining it transferring between myself and Gregory.

The man gasped. I had no doubt he realized the severity of my intentions. I had come with the intention of a dialogue. But as he attempted to play coy, giving me assurances that I was safe, I grew irate.

"You do not want them to find you," he assured me.

Slow and deliberate, I lifted my head, turning so I could see the side of his face. His hair had grown more salt than pepper, and his white sideburns bled into a perfect white beard. The man, despite being able to read my emotions, did not fully understand who he dealt with.

"They should be worried when I find them." There was no bravado, no false confidence. After dispatching two police officers for crimes against the city, I believed myself more than capable of dealing with any threat I encountered.

"I believe you need to calm yourself." Gregory had long since mastered the emotions of those around him. Like a warm blanket, the rage in my belly subsided, replaced by a sense of warmth and security. The man robbed me of my anger, and I struggled to be upset by his machinations.

"I hate you right now." Grumpy, it was the closest emotion to anger I could muster.

"Have you taken a moment to consider why I've been training you? Why I've been insistent on you learning to master your gifts?"

The words caught in my throat, my rapid-fire accusations swallowed like a bit of sour candy. In the months since we met, I never stopped to ponder the source of his generosity. The man offered me the one thing I desired, and without question, I accepted it, not caring what strings might be attached.

"I have not. There are a lot of questions I've overlooked that I would typically ask a complete stranger, especially another mentalist."

"I am partially to blame."

"You've been playing me all this time?"

Gregory nodded. "I lowered your inhibition and weaved a sense of comfort. It's what I do, Eleanor. This is my point. You're

powerful and you're able. But you have yet to masters your abilities. Until then, you're working with one arm tied behind your
back."

"You said they're coming for me," I turned on the bench,
facing Gregory now, "how do you know?"

"They seek out mentalists. They recruit them. Those who
refuse," the dread struck me like a mammoth wave. I gasped,
struggling to breathe. "Those who refuse them, Eleanor, they
murder."

"The killers?" I jumped off the bench, forcing my lungs to
suck in air. I imagined the wall erecting about my flame, warding
off Gregory's abilities.

With a deep breath, Gregory retracted the momentary slip-up.
"I apologize."

"If they send killers after those who refuse. Then those two
things were targeting people that the Society solicited?"

Gregory nodded. "Or mentalists they deem unworthy."

"Claudette?" I whispered. Edward? Had both of them been
offered a place amongst the Society's ranks? Gregory pulled the
rug out from underneath my feet. I had so many questions, but
none of them were for the man in front of me.

"Eleanor, be careful. If the Society has set its eyes on you,
there will be no running."

I had no intention of running. They had threatened to murder
people close to me, and because of that, I would see them driven
into the ground. I might have a moment of fear as I contemplated
their abilities, or how they might manipulate those around me.
The fear fell away as I remembered the police officers last night.
Those who crossed me should prepare for a hurricane of hurt.

"There's no reasoning with you." Gregory must still be
reading my emotions, feeling the confidence pouring out of my
mind.

"Many have tried. None succeed." I cocked my head to the
side as I thought of his involvement. Free from his manipulation,

I had a moment to ponder why he went out of his way to train a lone mentalist. "Why me? Why keep coming here to make sure I maximize my abilities?"

"Fear," he said. "Fear of the Society, and fear of you, Eleanor. You might be the only person with a gift capable of ensuring we are free of the Society. I'm an empath, a strong one perhaps, but I've squared off with a telepath before. I am no match, but you, your gifts are something unlike anything I've seen. You may prove the only opportunity for us all to be safe."

"Fear of me?"

"Wielded by any other, your gifts could be dangerous. What if you had a stain on your heart and felt the need to destroy rather than protect?"

I thought of the man I murdered. I did indeed have an ability that made me dangerous. What if I had no remorse? What if I decided that Bertolucci's empire would do better under my heel? There came a sense of power, but I felt no need to perpetuate the stranglehold he had over his minions.

"And if I crossed the line?"

"Then you'd be a lost cause. I wouldn't return day after day."

He made it sound simple, withholding his teachings. Underneath his words, I could sense a less than pleasant tone.

"You'd kill me."

He nodded. "Or at least I'd try."

Suddenly, a weight pressed down on my shoulders. The temptation to lose myself and treat the world as mine for the taking remained a point of contention between Edward and I. While I believed we had a responsibility to do good, he thought himself beyond the rules and laws of mortal men.

"I had a vision."

I no longer wanted to dwell on the what-if's or the idea that my mentor might someday find himself attempting to eliminate me. Instead, I wanted to focus on the training. There were things I could control, and those I could not. Right now, the Society must wait. These gifts were becoming more natural, but I understood Gregory's statements.

"Tell me," he patted the seat next to him. I sat, returning to our usual arrangement. I prepared to tell him about the church, the nun, the infant, and the young girl. If I were to become the savior for mentalists, I had much to learn.

"It started in a church…"

Frank was not the best sidekick. He could bark orders, but found it difficult to follow them. I grabbed him by the shirt, pulling him low. The big lug was built to trade blows with another man, not for stealth. I didn't want him to come, but he insisted. I didn't need to ask; he harbored guilt about giving me the name of the man attending group meetings.

"I will leave your ass here," I said.

Above the city, moving from one roof to the next, we had followed Matt for the last hour. He didn't hide in the shadows or look over his shoulder, fearful of being followed. I tried to speculate about his involvement with an organization bent on murdering mentalists, but I couldn't find a way the puzzle fit together.

The man walked along the street, glancing back and forth, confirming he hadn't been followed. He crossed the street and found himself at a restaurant, stepping inside. The awning over the front door revealed it to be a bakery. I couldn't imagine at this hour, anybody sought freshly made bread.

"What's he doing?" I whispered.

"We should wait," Frank said, "we have no idea what's going on inside."

I wanted to argue and throw caution to the wind, but Frank made me promise to keep my distance. Perhaps it was nothing, and the man truly needed baked goods in the middle of the night.

I doubted it, but it was the only excuse I could make to stay on the roof.

"Are you going to tell me where you got the jacket and mask?"

"A man in an antique shop gave me the jacket. He said I reminded him of his late wife."

"Of course he did." Frank found it entertaining how I found random storefronts in New York. From vintage stores selling worldly goods to Claudette's medicine shop, I had a knack for discovering the unique in this city.

"Emma Jean made me the mask. She might have made a few modifications to the jacket."

"Modifications?"

I reached behind my back, pulling one of the throwing knives free. I held it up for Frank to inspect. He made no attempt to take and examine it further.

"Does she know what you're doing at night?"

"Only you, Edward, and Claudette know. I know what you're thinking, Frank. I'm not going around sharing my secrets with everybody who will listen."

The knife slid into its holster in the back of the jacket. Frank cared sometimes too much. He didn't like that I dated Edward, or that Claudette wasn't forthcoming with her ability to know things beyond the ordinary. I hated to say it, but he thought like a human and didn't quite understand the world as we saw it, as mentalists *experienced* it.

"I worry," he said. "It's what dads do."

I smiled. He couldn't see it under the mask, but my cheeks turned bright red as my lips stretched across my face. "You're a good dad."

Seconds turned into minutes and we waited for some sign of what transpired below. I considered climbing down the fire escape and getting a closer look.

Gunfire.

Frank grabbed me by the shoulder, pulling me down. His hand continued applying pressure, ensuring I wouldn't stand up and peer over the ledge. Flattening himself on the roof, he belly crawled to the ledge, peering over to the bakery below. I followed suit.

Another shot fired, and we pulled back. I expected a fury of motion, men fleeing the bakery. Had the shots dispatched everybody inside? Were there no men left standing?

"What just happened?" I asked.

Frank didn't respond. We waited for another few minutes. Nothing about the street was out of the ordinary. I tried to recount how many shots they had fired. Was it five or six? How many bullets did that leave? Were the bangs the same? Did they come from one gun or were there multiple?

"Frank? What happened?"

"Six shots." Good to know I was right. "Three weapons. Three shots from the first, two others fired. The last shot came from the first weapon." Frank proved himself a useful sidekick. His training in the army might not prepare him for stalking men from the rooftops, but it did mean he knew guns. I valued his ability to fill in the gaps.

"We need to get out of here," I said.

"The police will be here any moment. Let's go."

Just like that, the only lead we had vanished. I found myself angry that we were no better off than we were when serial killers roamed the street. Though, after speaking with Gregory earlier, I still had to question Edward and Claudette about the Society. I wanted to know why both of them had neglected to mention the Society attempting to recruit them.

Chapter Fourteen

1942

"There is no need for you to sit on the fire escape."

Edward's studio apartment was small by any comparison. His bed covered one wall while a small kitchen table and a wall of cabinets covered another. The only doors led to the bathroom and the hallway. For a man who spent little time indoors, it was perfect. For the two of us, it verged on the side of cramped. I loved the man, but not enough to be on top of him day after day.

"We're in a fight."

"I suspected," he said while reclining in bed. The radio next to the bed was turned low, playing jazz music. Part of me wanted to ignore Gregory's insight and climb into bed with the man. The nightstand lamp made it easy to see his boyish features, a grin permanently fixed on his face.

It's anything but funny. I pushed the thoughts at him. I wanted him to not only hear my words but feel the annoyance hovering just beneath the surface.

"What did I do?"

Our relationship continued to be turbulent. I found him charming and being understood by another mentalist had its perks. However, we often fought over our philosophical differences. Up to this point, I believed we had put everything on the table, the good and the bad. Well, almost everything. I shouldn't be annoyed he had his own secrets, I continued to hide my abilities from him. This was different. This secret could end with both of us dead.

"You've been withholding information about the Society."

He didn't respond immediately. Edward always had words, an ability that more than often led to us arguing. His silence spoke volumes. He bit his tongue, waiting for me to provide the context, a ploy that made me even more nervous than when I first climbed his fire escape.

"They attempted to recruit you," I added.

"I'm quite desirable." He tucked his hands behind his head. The move accentuated his torso, his abs even more defined than normal. Edward knew I found him attractive, but this wouldn't slow me. Abs be damned.

"These people nearly killed you," I growled. "Me. They almost killed me. And you thought it wasn't worth mentioning?"

Eleanor—

"Don't," I said. "I'm not interested in you trying to charm your way out of this one. Tell me everything."

"How did you come by this information?"

"Edward!" I barked.

"Him? I should have guessed." Edward had no love for Gregory. I learned my boyfriend had a jealous streak when I first admitted to being trained by another mentalist. I quickly discovered my mistake as Edward went into a tirade. He believed himself more than capable, and I'm sure he had a trick or two up his sleeve, but I hadn't wanted our relationship to become mentor and mentee.

"Get over yourself and answer the question."

"The doctor, the man hosting the gala that night, he approached me. I thought he might be a mentalist until I scoured his mind. There was nothing of interest except a barrier I couldn't see past. I entertained his conversation."

"So you could find a crack in his thoughts."

"Exactly. No human has ever resisted me, not like that. It is the same barrier you have. A human isn't capable."

"The Society?"

Edward nodded. "He said that there was a group of people looking for people with my talents. He wanted me to join."

"You said no?"

"Eleanor, I would think by now you'd know I'm not a man who acts without weighing the benefits. Nothing he said sounded beneficial. I politely turned him down."

"Then you showed up at his event. Why?"

"You're quite the curious woman this evening."

"I wouldn't be curious if my boyfriend didn't see fit to hide information from me. Edward, you play a dangerous game."

Did he think by withholding the information he had leverage, a one-up over me? I had no qualms with admitting my partner's ego was problematic. We found a comfortable rhythm between us, but we always had tension. I wondered if this might be the source of it, or if it was something deeper.

"The man obviously had money. Between the suit and the watch, I knew his gala would be filled with pockets ripe for the picking."

I shook my head. "You're hiding something."

Seconds passed, and I had to shift my weight as the metal grate under my butt started to hurt. I had spent many evenings out here, enjoying the quiet noise of the city taking its last breath before sleeping. However, now I remained outside, making it known that this would not turn into a night of lovemaking and whispered affirmations.

"I wanted to know if they were there. I poked and prodded at the thoughts of every person in the room. They were all human, all but one."

"Me," I started to understand.

"That's when you ran. You thought I was one of them."

"You're not exactly an intimidating woman in a ball gown, but I handle anybody capable of hiding their thoughts with care. I emptied their pockets, payment for my time. Then I left."

"You fled."

"Perhaps," he tried to pass off the cowardice as self-preservation.

"Why hide this from me?"

"You're not the easiest person to date, Eleanor. Oh yes, by the way, the people who attempted to kill me might come for you. How much more complicated can our relationship get before you move on?"

Edward had a way with words. I couldn't tell if the talent came from being a telepath, or because he was indeed that charming. But his worry about me abandoning him was the first sincere statement of the evening. The man rarely discussed his feelings, but I found it endearing that he feared me leaving him. It almost provided a rationale for why he kept secrets.

"I haven't moved on."

"But will you now?" He tried to hide the concern, but I could tell he feared the answer.

"Not tonight," I said. I found the answers I wanted, but I had no intention of crawling inside his window and joining him in bed. This was our relationship, a series of events creating a gap, leaving us on opposite sides. Right now, I needed to process this bit of information, then I'd evaluate our relationship.

Be safe, Eleanor. The thought struck me as I climbed down the fire escape.

You too, my love.

Susan Lee had long since retired to bed. I appreciated the companionship of my roommate, but tonight I wanted to be alone. My head swirled as I attempted to process the new information. The Society, the same people who attempted to murder mentalists had solicited Edward. Meanwhile, Gregory continued to hide his association, but made his fear of them well known.

I believed we had a clue, a single man marked with the three wavy lines. We were close to a breakthrough, but I suspected the occupants of the bakery killed my only lead. I feared I'd realize how this puzzle fit together too late.

"A psychic scared of the future." I laughed. The irony was anything but lost. I hadn't feared the future for a long time. Now, I had no idea what might come my way. I needed answers, and even with the information from Edward, I found them just out of reach.

I gave myself a light tap on the face. Come on, Eleanor, you're missing something obvious. Gregory insisted the visions were the solution. The grand sweeping pictures of the future, broader than the ghosts and more revealing than the few minutes into the future I was used to seeing. I believed him, but I…

Closing my eyes, I rested my elbows on the ledge of the building. I imagined the flame in the palm of my hand. If I pushed hard enough, I might see ghosts of myself standing here night after night with Susan Lee. Like always, her ghost remained vacant, a question to solve for another time. But it wasn't the ghosts I needed, they wouldn't provide the answers I desired.

I inhaled deeply, going in through the nose and pushing it out slowly between parted lips. Edward had taught me to summon the flame, a visualization allowing me to control the ghosts. However, no matter how much I poured myself into the fire, it didn't stir the visions. Gregory suggested driving my emotions into the spark might be the wrong way to access my gifts.

I imagined an inferno, a circle of fire surrounding me, threatening to lean in and burn my skin. The ring grew until every direction burned bright. Instead of pushing into the fire, I inhaled. My imaginary hands dipped into the fire and I called it to me. Summoning a red-hot deity, flames licked my skin, drawing along my arms until it reached my shoulders.

I let down my walls, the barriers I held in place, saving me from turmoil. For a moment I swear I could see my father in the flame, rolling until the face transformed into my little brother. Benjie. My heart ached. I gasped aloud, tears rolling down my cheeks as I recounted the loss.

There was nothing separating me from the fire. Consumed in flame, drawing it into my body, I had glimpses into the future. Nazi flags waved back and forth, and thousands of black men and women marched holding signs, and a young man in a car lurched as his head exploded. The imaginary flame burned. With each thump of my heart, I fought the urge to cry out.

Then there was nothing.

The world faded away, leaving nothing but empty blackness. Startled, I couldn't focus on specifics. I hadn't been prepared for a vision to reveal itself. Lost in the emptiness, my abilities picked a vision for me. I jumped back as I realized the vision put a body at my feet.

The silhouette filled in details of the shirt and slacks until a faceless man rested on the ground. The red dot started just above his heart, spreading out until it became obvious the man had been shot. Blood poured out of the wound, pulsing in time with his heartbeat. I got down on my knees, examining the body, looking for clues as to the identity.

"Edward," I whispered.

The man's nose emerged from the face while the eyes sank into place. I recognized the boyish features. Hair sprouted from his head as glassy eyes appeared. There was no denying the man dying on the ground was Edward. I touched his face, shocked that I could feel his cooling cheek beneath my hand.

He stared into oblivion. Moments later, another version of me knelt at his head, sobbing at the sight of a dying Edward. She lifted his body, pulling him into her lap, one hand pressed on the wound as if she might stop the bleeding. Her other hand caressed his cheek, speaking too soft to hear. I tried to make sense of the scene. Somebody had shot Edward, and now I held him as he died.

I spun about, looking for the source of the shot, but found nothing but emptiness. The image had a familiarity to it. Just like Poppa and Benjie, I saw into the future and knew there was nothing I could do. Seeing the future came with rules I had yet to shatter. Fate refused to bend, to let me alter its plan. The fire contained within my body expelled at once, filling the space in a raging and blinding light.

Standing on the roof, my body tingled from head to toe. I gasped, running my hands along the stone, trying to discern if it was another vision or reality. I looked at my palms, worried the blood from the vision might have followed. They still felt tacky, covered in Edward's—

I pushed the thought from my mind. It might not have been the vision I wanted, but it very well could have been what I needed. I had never been able to force the future to unfold in front of me. I wondered if Gregory's philosophy about my walls shielding me from my pain was the solution? If I reached a new plateau with my gifts, perhaps it meant I could alter the future. Did the barrier set in place by destiny suddenly become malleable?

"Edward," I whispered. I might be mad, but I did not want him dead. I formulated a plan, a way to circumvent the future. There were no options. One way or another I would save the man I loved. My hands balled into fists and I slammed them down on the stone. My bones ached from the blow, reverberating all the way to my clavicle.

"No," I spat into the universe, "you can't have him."

I am Eleanor Bouvier. I will change the future.

Chapter Fifteen

1942

The world went mad while I slept.

Susan Lee sat at the kitchen table, her face stretched in horror as she flipped through the newspaper. Unlike usual, the radio didn't fill the tight space with jaunty tunes. Instead, a reporter spoke about the unfolding events in New York City. I found it odd that the routine we established for years had changed.

"What's wrong?"

Whatever atrocity had transpired captivated Susan Lee. Her eyes darted back and forth as she read the article. I sat down at the kitchen table, the scraping of the chair bringing her back to reality. She folded the paper in half, and then half again, sliding it across the table so I could read the headline.

"Citywide massacre?" That certainly grabbed the attention. It took a moment before my brain sorted through the awkward angle of the photograph. Two men were lying on the ground, guns just within reach, while another man found himself sprawled over a glass case of some sort. The caption underneath mentioned a bakery.

"Holy hell," I said. I was looking at the interior of the bakery

Frank and I had surveyed the night before. We knew something horrific had happened inside, but seeing it in the newspaper made it all the more terrifying.

"There's more," she said, as she switched the radio on.

I scanned the article. I flipped it over and continued reading. There were seven locations, all with similar acts of violence. I only recognized one of them, a tailor known for its mobster connections. Nowhere in the article did it mention Bertolucci or the fact the killings were linked to the mob.

"Do they know who did it?"

The radio let out a low tone before the reporter came on. "For those of you just tuning in, New York City has found itself under attack from unknown assailants. Last night, between the hours of midnight and two a.m., seven locations were burglarized and all occupants killed."

"It's horrible," Susan Lee said. I waved at the woman, trying to listen to the reporter.

"We are currently unaware if this is a tactic used by Germany to demoralize and defeat American citizens. However, we have confirmation that one of the bodies shares an identical tattoo with attackers from other locations. At this time we are unaware of the reasoning behind the massacre they caused. We will continue to report on the story as the police provide information."

"Damn," I said.

"Eleanor, language."

If ever there was a time to swear, it was now. While I slept, worried about a future in which a bleeding Edward died in my arms, New York went to war. Men with identical tattoos unleashed havoc on the mob. This meant the Society also waged war against the mob. I feared, in one night, this secret organization attempted to squash its only competition. However, they couldn't possibly understand Bertolucci's grasp on the city. With a good number of police officers in his pocket, the clandestine organization had their work cut out for them.

"Susan Lee," I reached across the table and rested my hand on hers. "I want you to be careful out there. New York is not a safe place right now."

"Me?" Her hand slid out from under mine and she rested it on my knuckles. "What about you? I work in a hospital and try to provide for our troops. I am as far removed from danger as it gets. You on the other hand," she gave me a stern look. "You have a knack for finding trouble."

I tried to recall if I slid away the jacket and mask. Did the woman have any inkling about my evening adventures? I had been incredibly careful, certain I wouldn't let anybody discover my somewhat ordinary life with the nurse.

"You hang out with a gym full of men. You're always coming in late from seeing Edward. Eleanor, you need to be more careful."

"Yes," I said, breathing a sigh of relief. "If I'm out late, I'll make sure Edward escorts me home from now on."

"Good. He could tolerate a few manners beaten into him."

I laughed. Susan Lee took a massacre and transformed it with the slightest bit of levity. She had a gift. With a single statement, I was reminded why I insisted we live together.

"I'll make an honest man out of him yet."

"You might be the only woman in the city capable of it," she said, reclining in her chair. Crossing her legs delicately, hands resting in her lap, she batted her eyes at me. "If he doesn't put a ring on your finger soon, I'm going to say it might be time to move on."

A ring?

I thought back to the vision, my ghost gripping the hands of a dying man. As she squeezed his fingers, I remembered there had been no ring. Perhaps Susan Lee had provided a solution so grand, not even fate could resist.

Chapter Sixteen

1942

I stalked my prey like an animal. Everybody in New York knew where to find Bertolucci in the evening. Overseeing his games of chance, he lorded over the fights like a king. I could have swept in, barged through the front door, posed as a patron, but I didn't want to cut off the head. I wanted to end Bertolucci's reign over New York City. Killing him would leave a vacuum, and one of his lieutenants could seize control. No, tonight I put an end to the mob.

I silently thanked the Society for waging war on the mobster. It had him calling on his men, gathering them together to create a protective barrier about him. The sheer number of mobsters circling the building indicated his fear. Where he typically had a half-dozen men about him, now, he had at least twenty. The hardest part was waiting, biding my time until I found an opening.

Hours ago, I wielded the ghosts unlike ever before. I pushed them forward, seeing into the future at first seconds, then minutes and even hours. They ventured away from the basement where Bertolucci played his twisted games, bankrupting those too fond of gambling. I found his car zigged and zagged, crossing from one street to the next, possibly trying to shake anybody who dared follow.

Now, I found myself outside a warehouse near the pier, a suitable place for mobsters to base their operations. They were more cautious, men hiding in the shadows, waiting for their master. Crates littered the space between the warehouse and the water. I hid far enough away to watch as men stepped in and out of shadows, guns hanging by straps from their shoulder.

I debated going after them, one at a time, thinning the herd. But my sidekick insisted I wait until Bertolucci was safely inside. If he suspected danger, he might turn around, and we'd never be able to follow. We needed Bertolucci's bravado to provide an opening. Frank hated this, but he understood it might be the only moment to be rid of the mobsters and the infection they spread throughout the city.

Frank only agreed to come in case the Society reared its head. I had begged him to stay behind, but he insisted, pulling the father card. Poppa could not possibly have predicted this predicament when he asked Frank to watch over me. The only concession had been Frank agreeing to run if the Society showed. I made it abundantly clear that humans stood no chance against those capable of reading their minds. I hoped I conveyed the severity of the situation. Knowing Frank, he'd only turn tail when we found victory.

Hours passed, and it was well past midnight when I heard the roar of an engine. The men in the shadows tucked themselves away, hiding in case it was another barrage of men with the three wavy lines.

Three cars appeared, rounding the corner. I ducked behind large barrels, staying in the shadows and out of sight. I peeked over the top to see the arrogant Bertolucci, taking inventory of the men by his side. One of them pointed toward the large crates scattered about. His lieutenant must be unveiling the number of men prepared to die for their leader. Satisfied, he walked from the car, entering a door to the side of the warehouse.

Another evening on the town, I see.

Curses. I had stopped to see Claudette and him earlier, warning them about the potential disaster about to unfold. I made certain they knew the Society had been behind the attacks. Claudette promised to stay indoors, but Edward required more convincing.

Edward, you swore you'd stay out of this.

If I remember correctly, I said I wouldn't leave my apartment this evening.

I loved the man, but he had learned which buttons to press. *I'll get back to you.*

You know where to find me if you need help.

He couldn't pluck thoughts from my mind unless I wanted, but he had discovered he could still insert himself. The tiny voice echoing in my mind vanished. His feelings were hurt. He wanted to remind me he could be standing at my side. I had considered it, but I couldn't predict how he might dispense his own brand of justice. At least Frank and I agreed on a policy to dispatch the men.

The ghosts came with the slightest nudge. They were eager to show me the dangers that awaited. Brighter than their owners, I could see the hiding spot of every mobster. Tucked away behind crates, palettes, and oil barrels, they waited. They should be scared, but not of the Society.

I pulled up the mask, securing it to my face. The charcoal crumbled in my hand before I dragged it over my eyes. I had taken on four men at once without much difficulty. The element of surprise was on my side. I would need it tonight. The moment they discovered somebody singling them out, we'd have to chase Bertolucci. I did not want the snake slithering from his nest.

Frank's ghost moved slowly, close to the ground. He carried a revolver at his back and a knife in his boot, but neither of those weapons compared to his hand-to-hand combat. The ghost approached a henchman, and without the slightest sound, Frank cracked the man's neck.

It had begun.

I watched the three ghosts closest to me. Paying special attention to their heads, I waited until all three looked away. I moved from behind a crate to a long shipping container. This time, I looked above and behind. I wouldn't allow myself to be surprised like last time.

I inhaled deeply, preparing myself for the blood about to be spilled. Inching along the container, I reached behind my back, securing one of the throwing knives. Fingers snaking around the blade, I spun around the edge of the crate. Grabbing the man's head, I drove the blade into his neck. His body tensed, and hardly a sound slipped from between his lips.

I held him upright, dragging him backward out of sight. Laying him on the pavement, I took a moment to comprehend how many more times I'd repeat the maneuver this evening. If I let my mind wander, I'd begin thinking about their families, wives and children losing their fathers. No, I couldn't dwell. These men attempted to strangle the life from the people of New York. I had to stand firm in my conviction. Their souls could haunt me as I drifted off to sleep. I needed to finish the job I started.

Frank had reached the third mobster. I had always known the military trained him to be ruthless. He fought their programming every day in the gym. To see how easily he slipped into the role, I feared he might fall victim to his vices. With every man killed, did he grow closer to needing a drink to sleep at night? I prayed that I didn't shove him back into a world he couldn't escape.

My fingers tightened around the blade as I caught sight of a moving shadow. The world slowed as I allowed the ghosts to return. A man holding a gun hid behind a stack of oil barrels, now and then peeking around the side. The gun pointed toward the ground, assuring me he hadn't spotted either of us.

If I hurled the blade, aiming for the eye, I could dispatch him quickly. I didn't dare summon my own ghost. I didn't want to see the outcome of a missed throw and be bound to a future I couldn't change. It was a sick game with fate, and for now, I knew how to prevent locking myself into an unchangeable future.

Tiptoeing, I worked my way behind his ghost. With his back to me, I almost found it to be unfair. I stepped behind him. Grabbing his face with my left hand, tilting his head to expose the neck. I slid the knife into the soft tissue. I didn't voice it, but I thought of a silent apology to those loved by this man, this corpse.

His body twitched. The bang startled me, forcing me to throw the man's body against the barrels. It took a moment for me to realize his finger had tightened on the trigger. I could hear the shouting as the men called to one another.

"Johnny?" yelled a man. "Tino?"

Neither man replied. I didn't know if it had been Frank or me who killed Johnny and Tino, but I knew the men were now on alert. A hint of fear crept into my mind, worry that they would discover Frank, or that one of the men would gun me down. I tried to quiet it with the image of me lying on the floor as an old woman, dead. I knew when I died, and tonight was not that night.

The assurances were shoved into the flame. I imagined the fire erupting, splashing into the air until it covered my skin. I pulled back to see an image of myself consumed, hair composed of beautiful strands of fire. Mentalist. Psychic. The confidence set the hair on my arms on end. I felt untouchable, invincible as my abilities poured out.

I could see the ghosts, except these were no longer transparent apparitions. Their perfectly formed bodies were solid, stretching seconds and minutes into the future. No longer did I have to guess how far into the future I was seeing. An internal clock pinpointed their place in the timeline. One-point-two seconds. Two-point-eight seconds. I simply knew.

I reached behind my back and pulled the second blade free. Frank might need to hide, dodge between the shadows. I didn't need protection as I hid between the ghosts. I stood just outside the timeline and I planned on taking advantage of it.

One of the ghosts held the gun at his waist, coming around the side of the barrels. I stepped into place, waiting for the owner's face to come into view. I kicked, striking the man's gun, knocking it free. By the time he turned to face his attacker, I leaned in with the knife, lunging. It sank easily above his Adam's apple, piercing the spot where his brain met his spine.

Another ghost emerged from behind crates twenty feet away. I watched as it squeezed the trigger. Six phantom bullets flew by. I walked forward, taking slight steps to the right and left. As he fired, I listened to the bits of lead whistle by, close enough to make me flinch.

"What the fuck," he said. To him, I must appear indestructible, able to absorb bullets. With a flick of the wrist, I sent the blade flipping end over end. I didn't need to watch to know I struck his eye.

"There, I see him." In a game of cat and mouse, they thought themselves the cats. They had yet to realize each time they stepped from the shadows, they became inferior mice. Bertolucci should have considered training his men to work as a unit. Perhaps if Frank ruled the mob, they'd have learned to work as a team. Together, I might not be able to dance between their bullets and kill them one by one.

Maybe.

I no longer hid. I watched as the ghosts of both men raised their guns. A spray of bullets filled the air. I ducked low, spinning to the left. I stopped short and watched the bullet pass inches from my face. Seeing moments into the future, I managed to maneuver between each shot, expertly bending and folding my body.

"It's a woman." One of the men shouted. "Mickey, it's a fucking woman."

Somehow being a woman gave them a bolster of confidence. I ran toward them. The man on the left raised his gun. Pulling the trigger only resulted in empty clicking. I jumped, slamming both of my heels into the man's chest. His companion turned his gun, hoping for an easy shot. My back slammed on the concrete. I rolled to my side, kicking him in the knee.

Shots fired in the air as he fell.

His ghost reached back, balling his fist. I pulled my head out of the way, yanking at his sleeve so he buckled over at the waist. Spinning my legs gave me enough momentum to sit upright. I rolled onto his back, wrapping my arm around his neck. I squeezed, using my other arm as leverage. The man tried to shake me, but I refused to let go. His movements grew sluggish. Finally, he collapsed onto his side. I held on, needing him dead, not unconscious.

Another shadow walked forward, and I summoned the ghosts. I breathed a sigh of relief as Frank's specter held his hand out, offering me a hand.

"Inside?" he asked.

I took the gun from the dead man. Frank walked just behind me. I didn't need to see his face clearly to know the Frank I loved had been replaced by a soldier. This was why I hadn't wanted him to come. I couldn't imagine the number of meetings he'd have to attend before he started to atone for his sins this night.

I squeezed the trigger, firing at the cars. The automatic weapon was far from accurate. Sparks flew out from the doors, but eventually, I managed to hit the tires. Popping and wheezing filled the air. I threw the gun to the side, satisfied there was no easy way to escape this evening.

I waved Frank forward. "Inside."

Careful, my dear.

Edward whispered in the back of my head. I wondered if he could sense the power rolling off my body as I neared the warehouse door. If he could sense my abilities heightened, could the Society? Were they watching, allowing me to do their dirty work? Part of me hoped they would arrive to find me standing victorious over New York's underworld. I wanted them as scared as the men inside the warehouse.

Inside, two men waited, their guns raised. As my ghost walked into the space, I could see a dozen men surrounding Bertolucci. The warehouse contained rows of shelves filled with crates and boxes. They scattered the floor, waiting to be loaded into one of the several trucks parked inside. I couldn't make out what the warehouse was intended for, just another generic building pushing inventory from one location to the next.

I almost laughed when I caught sight of the two policemen from the previous night. He believed himself safe, surrounded by weapons and minions. The man's ego gave him assurances it couldn't fulfill.

I pushed at the door with my foot and rolled to the side. Gunfire rattled off, echoing in the warehouse. Frank had gone to find another way in the building. Twenty men hid inside, ready to kill me. Twenty henchmen prepared to put their life on the line for a tyrant. Twenty and Bertolucci made twenty-one. Tonight that would be the exact number to die.

I rolled into the entrance, knife poised to strike. It only took a moment for me to decide the man loading ammunition into his gun would die second. I hurled the blade. I'd admire the precision later. Gurgling on blood, one henchman fell to the ground. I charged in, dropping my shoulder. I hit him in the gut, knocking him in one direction while his gun skid in the other.

"A fucking broad," he cursed as he pushed himself upright.

I tried to kick him under the jaw. The mobster moved faster than expected, catching my foot. Pulling hard, he turned my leg, trying to snap my hip out of place. Spinning with the turn, the toe of my other boot nailed him in the temple. I fell onto my stomach, brought my leg in and donkey kicked him in the face.

I crawled until I grabbed the knife, tearing it from the first man's throat. His companion grabbed me by the hair, using it for leverage. Men and their incessant need to grab a woman's hair. I reached back, driving the tip of the knife into his hand. He let go. I pivoted on my heel, the blade stretched out. It slipped through the skin of his neck and I added another dead man to my tally.

"I want them alive," screamed Bertolucci. The man's audacity would be his undoing. Even if he had the ability to kill me, he should have at least tried. Handicapping his men would make this easier. The king of New York City was only minutes from losing his crown and his head.

The knife slid into the holster on the back of my jacket. I grabbed the fallen gun and scooted behind a stack of crates. This was larger than the guns Frank taught me to shoot. The circular container underneath housed the ammunition. They fired, but their accuracy left something to be desired. Frank swore by his pistol. But right now, I had eighteen more henchmen that needed to die before I felt comfortable facing their kingpin.

I dropped to my knees behind a row of crates. Their ghosts put them right where I wanted. Even if I didn't land a killing shot, I needed fewer men with guns hunting me. I waited three seconds and jumped from my hiding spot. I skid along the pavement, pulling the trigger. Both men twitched as I struck them in their torsos. I didn't wait for them to fall before I climbed to my feet and ran toward a large box truck.

The goons traveled in packs, in some misbegotten belief that numbers would save them. I could see their ghosts creeping along the side of the truck, and they'd reach me in just under ten seconds. But there was no need wait as I got down on my hands and knees, scooting partway under the truck. I squeezed the trigger, aiming for their feet and legs.

They fell, and I continued to hold the trigger. All three, dead. The gun stopped firing. I tried the trigger again, unsure if it jammed or I exhausted my ammo.

Hands grabbed at my legs, pulling me from under the truck. He flipped me over without effort. While I mocked Bertolucci for his arrogance, I realized I too shared this flaw. How many times would it take before I started looking at my surroundings on all sides before rushing in?

I tried kicking the man, but his time working out had given him far more muscle than his shirt revealed. He grabbed me by the jacket. I tried reaching for the knife, but pinned behind my back, I couldn't wiggle it free.

"A scared little girl." The man's voice fit him, low and mumbly. He grabbed my jacket and lifted me off my back. The handle of the knife fit perfectly into my palm. I dragged it along his forearm. For any other man, it would have caused him to let go, but this brute treated it as nothing more than a superficial wound.

"Ha, not so quick—"

He brought me closer, preparing to slap me across the face. I plunged the knife into his chest. Too dumb to die, my cheek stung as he raked his knuckles across my face. Blood bubbled over his lip, dripping onto his vest. Touching his face, he stared at the blood, unsure of what it meant. I held his hand. Bracing one foot on his waist, I lifted the other, driving my heel on the knife.

The blade vanished inside his body and I cursed at losing my second blade of the evening. Another second and he let me go, landing with a thump. He fell, still not convinced he was dying. I almost pitied the stupid man. At what point did a person accept death as inevitable and embrace it? I noted the irony before I reached for his gun.

"If you want your friend to live, you might consider revealing yourself."

"Frank?" I whispered.

I forced the ghost from my body. Stepping around the truck, I moved forward until I could see two men standing over an unconscious Frank. I had been so busy, I forgot my sidekick. At some point, even with training, I had to remember he was still only a man. I wouldn't risk him for this vendetta. The ghosts were recalled as I moved alongside the truck toward a clearing where Bertolucci and his men waited.

"I'll come out if you promise not to kill him."

"I'm not some common thug."

"Then you're an uncommon thug."

"Perhaps, but if you want this man to live. You'll turn yourself in."

"How do I know you won't kill him anyway?" I knew the answer. I had no assurances. He could very well put a bullet between my eyes the moment he saw me. Then who would be alive to save Frank?

"I'm coming out."

It was the last thing anybody expected. I raised my hands over my head, ready to turn myself in. No, scratch that. There was one more thing I could do.

I took my time, small steps forward. I could see Frank on the ground with two mobsters standing over him, guns in hand. His body moved slightly as he breathed. They hadn't killed him. I might be able to kill one or two, but with so many holding guns, there was no way I'd be able to survive long enough to reach Bertolucci.

I need your help.

Chapter Seventeen

1942

Did you ask for my help?

Even in the face of death, Edward infuriated me. He wanted it spelled out, crystal clear that I needed him to save the day. I feared inviting him would lead to the gunshot that killed the man. I wanted him safe, away from danger, but I couldn't risk Frank's life for my own ego.

Edward, I need you.

He didn't respond, but I knew the man found satisfaction in the request. I needed to buy us as much time as possible. How long would it take him to get from his apartment to the docks? Ten minutes? Fifteen? Even if he found a cab, I didn't believe he'd be able to arrive in time. I secretly hoped the man had more tricks up his sleeve.

Bertolucci stood with a police officer on either side. The man took a sick satisfaction in appointing men who should be stopping him. The goon at my side dragged me forward. I struggled, trying to shake free from his grip. The man on my right punched me in the stomach. I fought to keep from hurling on the warehouse floor. His men already believed me less than, and I refused to give them the pleasure of seeing me grimace.

"So you're the one who orchestrated this?"

"I have a lot of free time on my hands." The more he talked, the longer I stayed alive. I needed him to threaten me. The longer he took, the more likely Edward would rush through the door and save me and Frank.

"You hired the hit on my men?"

"I'm not the only one who wants you dead." It was a fact. An ego as large as his would talk.

"What do you know?"

I must have taken too long to answer. He nodded toward the man on my left. Kicking behind my knee, I fell. The two men held me on the shoulders, pressing down so I couldn't stand. I didn't need knives to know that with a quick backhand, I could nail them both in the groin. I needed to bide my time, observing, looking for weak points in Bertolucci's men. Koji might almost be proud.

"I know enough."

Bertolucci unbuttoned his jacket. He slid it off, tossing it across one of the crates just behind him. He started with the cuffs, unfastening them and rolling up his sleeves.

"Do you know what it takes to run a city?"

Good, he wanted to talk. I feigned struggling as the men's hands tightened on my shoulders. Give him the impression he held all the cards.

"I started in the boroughs with nothing. I fought tooth and nail. Since I was a child, I've always been a scrapper." Killer, he didn't need to say it, I could tell the meaning was implied. "I've taken on the coppers, and I've bought off politicians. And you think you can come in here and take it away?"

He leaned forward, brushing a hand against the mask. I thought he might pull it down, revealing my identity. Bertolucci swung, the back of his hand striking me along the face. It might not leave a bruise, but it stung enough to make me hiss. Be weak, show them fragility. I started formulating a plan.

"And in one night, they knocked you down a peg," I added a laugh. I needed to threaten his manhood. A woman mocking him would make his blood boil. *Anger leads to impulse, and in turn, leads to mistakes.* Koji, I owed him dinner for a month after this.

"Who are they?"

"They call themselves the Society." There was no point in hiding the information. If he died tonight, the Society won. If he survived, then I might pit the two organizations against one another. In a different light, the mob might have been my greatest allies in defeating the Society. I hoped I put my money down on the right side.

"You're one of them?"

I shook my head. "I'm freelance. I just hate you."

He reached out, snaking his finger inside my mask, brushing his thick finger against my nose. I forced a smile as the man pulled the cloth down. It hugged my neck, and I had a moment to revel in the confusion on Bertolucci's face. For a man proclaiming he knew everything about New York, he never realized one of his patrons might challenge him.

"The casino?"

I nodded. "I'm glad to see I left an impression."

He took a step back, trying to process the information. It might be childish, but I took satisfaction in unnerving the man. I had no idea if he recalled the night Edward saved me from his goons. Did he know a telepath influenced his men, making them incapable of carrying out their orders to carry me out back and kill me?

"I bet you feel foolish now."

Smack. *Anger lead to mistakes.* "You stole my money. And now you come for me like you're a boss?"

"It's easy to win in your casino when I can see the future."

Sure, let's throw out as much information as I can to drag out this interlude. I wish Edward would snake his way into my thoughts and tell me how much longer I needed to stall the mobster. Edward might save the day, but he'd do it on his own terms. There would be much yelling between us later.

"The woman is insane," Bertolucci cried. The surrounding men laughed. I knew there was no way they'd believe me. I didn't need them to believe, I needed them to see me as crazy. People get reckless around those deemed less than stable. I knew from experience.

"And yet, I walked away each night with my pockets full of your money. I killed a dozen of your men."

He eyed Frank. He believed my hired muscle had done the heavy lifting. Part of him. He took a slight step back, wary. Some part of him processed the information, and he found something irrefutable, some bit he couldn't explain. I rarely shared my secret and watching the confusion on his face, I confirmed why. Was I crazy, or was there a morsel of truth behind my words.

"Why is the Society after me?"

I wanted to shrug, but the men refused to let up. "Perhaps they don't like you. I hardly know you and I think you're scum."

I winked at the tall officer. The man scowled. "I see you found your pants."

The fear weaving through each of the men, I understood why Edward savored his superiority. There was something downright delicious about watching these men terrified of poor little me.

"If you don't tell me why, I'll kill you."

"You're going to try to put a bullet between my eyes either way. There's really—"

He smacked me again. I turned with the blow. Two men hovered over Frank. I caught sight of his eyes blinking. There were five within reach of me now. Another dozen hid somewhere in the warehouse, guarding the doors to ensure nobody else entered.

"Try? The dame thinks she is in charge." Bertolucci laughed. His cronies followed suit. None of them believed me a threat.

"She thinks she can see the future." Bertolucci leaned in, getting close enough that I could smell the spices from dinner on his breath. "What do you see in the future?"

"You don't want to know."

The smile faded, his top lip quivering in anger. "I think I do."

"Frank," I said loud enough they could all hear. "I'm going to kill them."

"You and what army?"

The ghosts flooded the room.

"I am the army."

Chapter Eighteen

1942

My forehead bashed against his nose. Arms shot forward and then slammed backward, hitting the groins of the men on either side. Bertolucci straightened, backing up. As the pressure on my shoulders lessened, I reached for the goon's pant leg, snatching his small pistol.

The two officers behind Bertolucci raised their guns. But I stepped in close to their boss, making sure they couldn't fire without killing the man who paid them. I turned, pulling the trigger. One shot, then two. The man on the left collapsed and with another shot into the dome of his companion, I had two dead mobsters.

Bertolucci attempted to wrap his arms around me. I drove my heel down onto the bridge of his foot. Slamming my head back, I grazed his already gushing nose. I tried not to think about the amount of blood coating my hair. The ghosts, I needed to focus on the ghosts. There wasn't much time before the gunfire summoned the rest of his troops.

I checked over my shoulder, around Bertolucci, to see the ghost of a slender mobster stepping forward, pulling his boss out of the way as he fired. I reached into my pocket, sliding the brass knuckles over my fingers. As the officer stepped in, pointing the gun at my head, I moved into an uppercut. The knuckles connected with his jaw and two teeth went flying as his jaw snapped shut.

"Eleanor, behind you."

I needed to remember to look behind me. Moving forward in time, I often forget I couldn't see the world unfold behind me. Koji would have a field day when he found out I wasn't protecting myself on all sides.

The gun pressed against my skull. He hesitated, unsure if his boss wanted me dead. I tilted my head out of the way. The bang of the gun so close to my ear forced a scream. I went tone deaf in one ear. I thrust an elbow back, then turned into the man. Face to face, I grabbed his gun arm, leaned forward and rolled the man over my hip. Hitting the ground, I twisted his hand until I held the gun. Two shots in the chest and he stopped moving.

I watched the ghosts. The two officers stepped forward, firing. My ghost stepped forward, attempting to duck and roll past the shots. Jumping to her feet, I watched the hole blow through my ghost's chest. Bertolucci had freed his weapon and with a single shot, he killed me.

I died.

I pushed the fire, slowing time. Stoking the flames, the entire room ground to a halt. I watched another version of my ghost roll to the side. Then another, falling backward. Multiple versions of my ghost attempting to survive. Each version ended with a bullet plunging into my body.

Multiple versions. Never had I been able to see variations of the future. In a moment of survival, I found my abilities running rampant. I pushed the fear and the anger into the flame. The woman in my imagination was nothing more than fire, soaring above the ground as heat caused the air about her to ripple.

I counted seventeen versions before I found the only one

where I didn't die immediately. Time flowed normally as I stood, hands held above my head. The gun fell to the side, landing on one of the dead men.

"It's over, Frank," I said. "I die no matter how this turns out."

Were there more versions? Could I see infinite possibilities? Given enough time, I might be able to solve this problem. I might walk out of here alive. But if I died, the vision of me on a plush carpet, bleeding from a bullet wound would never come to fruition. Did the ghosts lie to me? Had something about them changed? Something about me?

Bertolucci raised the gun, pointing it directly at my face. The fury on his face revealed that he no longer cared for answers. The man wanted to kill. I had run out of time.

The tall officer cocked his weapon, slowly, deliberate. I wondered if he'd put a bullet in my corpse just to gain a sense of satisfaction. His chubby compatriot however looked dazed, confused at the events unfolding about him. I couldn't imagine them working together.

The chubby man pulled out his gun. Late to the party, he pointed it at the tall officer, squeezing the trigger. Bertolucci jumped, turning around to see the source of the gunfire. I chopped him across the throat with my left hand, going for the gun with my right. I ignored the tall officer shooting the chubby man. Chaos erupted as gunfire filled the warehouse.

I struggled with the gun. Forcing it to point away from me. The mobster proved stronger than I anticipated. Even unable to breathe, he pushed me away with one arm, forcing the gun from my grip. He jumped back, ready to shoot me in the chest.

"You asked for help." The words came out in a hoarse croak. It might have been Bertolucci's voice, but it was Edward's demeanor.

"About damned time," I said.

As quickly as the gunfire started the warehouse returned to its eerie quiet. The only man remaining, Bertolucci. I snatched the gun out of his hand, fearful that Edward couldn't deliver.

"Did you influence them all?"

"I did." Edward's voice. I turned to see my savior. The boyish charm I found so attractive had vanished, replaced with a devilish smirk. He had been given carte blanche to dispatch the mob as he saw fit. I imagined he whispered in each of their heads, demanding they kill their friends.

For a moment, I feared Edward and his newfound abilities.

"Only one remains."

I stared at Bertolucci. His face no longer revealed a powerful man. Instead, fear spread across his face. I saw a glimpse into a terrifying future. Mentalists versus humans. The fear on his furrowed brow would be repeated on the face of every human who knew about our existence.

Edward reached for my hand, sliding the gun from my grip. I reached out, needing even a simple hand holding. I wanted to know I wasn't alone.

Edward lifted his hand, pulling back the hammer. There was no hesitation, no moment to ponder. The hammer fell and the last bang sounded through the warehouse. I watched as Bertolucci's chest thumped, red splattering along his white shirt. Even in death, the mobster remained arrogant. He clutched his chest, looking at his hands, refusing to accept his fate.

"No."

The single word escaped his lips before he fell to his knees. I came tonight to create this very scene. I knew only one of us would walk away. And yet, somehow, seeing the cold demeanor of Edward, it felt off. Was it hypocrisy to believe Bertolucci shouldn't have died by Edward's hand? Was it childish to think the mobster should have been given a fighting chance?

I tried not to think of the carnage Edward unleashed in just a few minutes. My boyfriend had come to my rescue. I had to focus on the good. In my time of need, Edward had committed a heinous act to save me. I didn't want to question his intent, but part of me, some tiny piece of my heart feared Edward.

"Thank you," Frank said.

"My pleasure," Edward responded.

That might be the problem. I came here out of a sense of duty to New York. I was willing to risk myself to make the streets a safer place for all. Had I opened Pandora's box? Was Edward the embodiment of war? I feared the answer.

Chapter Nineteen

1942

The walk to his apartment had been a silent one. I had time to think about the blood and the gore. Washing it down the drain made it impossible to ignore the savagery I'd unleashed in a single night. I had stopped muggers and protected women of the night, but I had never waged a war.

The pink water swirled about in the drain. I didn't forget about Frank or Edward's involvement, but I had led the charge. Me, a woman from the Midwest. I had taken this curse and used it for something good. I nearly hurled as I thought about the wet sounds of my knife sinking into the man's chest. Hurled then cheered.

Part of me reveled in the victory. Because of me, New York City was one step closer to being a safe place. When the troops returned, they'd find the streets welcoming, their shops still open. I shut off the water, grabbing a towel off the rack.

Emotions clashed as I toweled my hair. Part of me feared the woman I had become, while part tried to understand the next task for my vigilante alter ego. I tried to silence the thoughts, to push them away. I wrapped the towel around my breasts, the soft cloth reaching my thighs. There was no coping right now, I needed a distraction. Anything to stop thinking about the future.

Opening the door, Edward stood there with his hand raised, prepared to knock.

"I was going to check in on you."

I shoved him back. Confused, he started to speak. I grabbed him by the button-down shirt and pulled myself to him. I pushed my lips against his, biting his lower lip. Yes, Edward was many things, including a suitable distraction. Feeling his eagerness against my thigh, I was certain he wouldn't mind being used.

I ripped open the shirt. Surprised, he let out a slight laugh. The humor in his face melted, replaced by something less than boyish. The last button admitted defeat, flying toward the bathroom. I pulled the shirt off his shoulders, holding his arms in place. There was no denying how incredibly sexy he could be.

"I didn't—"

No talking. The thought wasn't a suggestion, it was a demand. The fact Edward stopped showed just how badly he wanted this. I rested my hands on his pecs, letting my fingernails trail down his smooth chest and to his abs. Following the lines of his body, I traced around his belly button before I reached the waistband of his trousers.

He jerked the towel from my body, leaving me naked. He bit his lower lip as he stared. His eyes traveled from my feet to my breasts. He reached for my waist, pulling me close, kissing along my jaw until he reached my lips. Edward could infuriate me, but with a passionate kiss, nothing mattered except removing his slacks.

Are you okay?

It was a loaded question, and one I wish he hadn't asked. No, I wasn't okay, I had been through hell this evening. I nearly lost my father, the one man… I couldn't dwell on it. Now I stood naked in front of a man I feared could be shot.

Eleanor, what is it?

His words were genuine, filled with concern. I rested my hands on his chest. He held both of my hands, giving them a light squeeze. Edward had his tender moments. His hands dwarfed mine, nearly making them invisible. I stared at his ring finger. Susan Lee's comment hovered in the back of my mind. Fate be damned.

Marry me.

I could almost hear fate gasp. This is how I'd cheat the system. I'd bend the future even if it killed me. There was no way I'd let him die.

Edward made no move. He didn't blink. I nearly repeated myself when his hands tightened on mine. His hand slid along my waist, pulling me close. It started with a shimmer in the eyes and spread to the smirk. I had no doubt that those boyish good looks had gotten him in trouble more than once.

"Yes."

I imagined a ring on his finger and a rushed wedding. We'd act with haste. He'd think it was a whirlwind romance. I never imagined myself marrying, but if it meant he'd live, I could survive.

"Mr. Eleanor Bouvier, it has a certain ring to it."

He laughed. Cupping my behind, he lifted me up, so that I wrapped my legs around his waist. Kissing me with reckless abandon, he turned and walked to the bed. When his shins hit the end, he tossed me onto the mattress. I shot up, reaching for the button on his trousers.

"Not yet," he said. Pushing me back on the bed, he crawled over my body. He kissed my lips and moved down my cheek to the spot where my neck connected to my shoulders. I squirmed as the scruff of his cheek brushed my skin. He gently touched my skin with his lips as he moved down my sternum.

He paused. My body tightened in anticipation. He kissed along my breast until his mouth hovered over the nipple. With a flick of his tongue, I bit down on my lower lip. He teased, knowing full well what I really wanted. He lowered his mouth, teeth bearing down on the skin. My back arched and my nails dug into the sheets. It only amplified as he rolled my other nipple between his fingers.

There were many things we could argue about, topics effectively deemed off-limits. Sex, however, was not a topic we shied away from. Predicting my body's reaction, the mentalist had the ability to transform a simple act into an evening affair.

He slid down my body until his knees were resting on the floor. He grabbed me by the legs, pulling me down the bed until my legs hung over the side.

I opened my eyes, and the apartment had vanished. We were in the middle of the Metropolitan Museum of Art. In the grand hall, the walls were lined with paintings by European masters. Patrons moved through the space, admiring the artwork, oblivious to the sexual act taking place in the middle of the room. I wanted to scold him, not for his decision to conjure the museum, but for bring the people with it.

My anger diminished as he kissed the inside of my thigh. I no longer cared about the wooden table under my back, or the young couple talking nearby. Right now, all I wanted was Edward to stop with the foreplay.

Stop teasing. There was no way I didn't shout the command at the man.

He stopped teasing.

Yes, Eleanor Valentine.

Chapter Twenty

1931

The medicine did nothing to drive away the ghosts. The pills slowed my thoughts, making it hard to find my words. For the first few weeks, I prayed they might be the solution. However, the ghosts persisted, uncaring how many pills I swallowed. Foggy and unable to rally against their constant appearances, I decided it was best to have my wits about me. If not for the ghosts, then for the other patients who seemed to attack one another frequently or break into fits and tantrums.

They had turned the lights off nearly three hours ago, but there was still light shining through the large windows in the room. The bunks held beds for all the women, dozens sleeping in rows. Occasionally one would wake, screaming at invisible foes. I wondered if they could see the ghosts. Perhaps I wasn't alone, and similar demons haunted them.

The orderly would return shortly, doing his rounds as he walked up and down the aisles between cots. My ghosts weren't the most terrifying thing in the hospital. This staff had a sickness about them. The doctor hired men who found pleasure in victimizing the women, and the nurses were just as evil. For individuals sworn to help the sick, they treated us more like specimens.

I reached under my pillow and made sure I grabbed all three of the tiny pills. After six weeks of observing the patients, I learned not everybody played by the doctor's rules. Hiding the pills between my gums and lip, I pocketed my meds when the orderlies dispensed medication. They were too busy attempting to make me speak, to test my reluctance to use my voice to notice I spit the pills into my hand and saved them for later.

In a psychiatric ward, meds served as currency. The patients traded their pills, chasing highs, or seeking a chance to reach oblivion. If I came here, driven mad by the ghosts, then perhaps I wasn't the only one. I confirmed twelve of the women with invisible friends did not see the ghosts. I had one left and prayed she confirmed their existence. I needed to know I wasn't alone, and that being locked away served a purpose.

I slid off the bed, taking care to avoid the loose floorboard. I tiptoed, staying low as I went. I reached Virginia. Sleeping soundly, I touched the side of her face, giving her a slight tap. She snorted as she woke, pushing away, trained to fear her captors. I held up my fingers, shushing her. A quick glance over my shoulder ensured there were no orderlies in the room.

"What do you want?" she whispered.

I reached into my pocket and pulled out a folded sheet of paper. Careful to not tear it, I held it up to catch the lamps used to keep the grounds illuminated. She wiped her eyes, blinking several times before she took the paper.

"Do I see ghosts? Who wants to know?"

I held up three white pills. Virginia's eyes went wide, and she peeked over my shoulder to make sure the coast was clear. She snatched the pills from my hand and swallowed them immediately.

"I do," she whispered. "They're everywhere." I held my breath, hoping that perhaps I wasn't alone. I needed to know that somebody else could see them. Even if there was only one, it would prove this wasn't an illness hounding me. One, I only required one.

"I see ghosts all the time. Dead people." My heart sank. "My husband talks to me. I hear our cat too."

I reached out to take the paper and our hands touched. A rush of black swallowed me. The room and the cots vanished, as did the sounds of the dozens of snoring women. I was alone in a vault of darkness. Alone except for *them*, even here the ghosts found me.

The hair on my arm stood on end, threatening to pull itself free. I spun about, watching the faint images fade in and out of sight. Unlike their usual counterparts, the ghosts here were of people I had never seen. These visions were the scariest, showing me events far into the future, terrible things I knew were to be true, but I had no ability to change. The last one had been of Benjie falling through the ice, a terror lived twice.

It started blurry and steadily cleared. The middle of the room held an operating table with bright lights chasing away the shadows. I had never seen this room, but I assumed it was part of the hospital. The dirty secrets about the basement were whispered about amongst the women, horrible, outlandish experiments performed by the doctor. As I stared at the bloody floor, I knew the whispers were closer to the truth than any suspected.

I held my breath, waiting for the people to populate the horrific scene. I wrapped my arms around my torso as Virginia appeared, strapped to the table. Leather bands circled her wrists and ankles with another clenching her head in place. Her spine bowed as she tried to wrestle free from her restraints. Her mouth distorted in terror and I'm sure she screamed at the top of her lungs. The silent cries made my skin crawl. I feared I'd vomit.

A nurse came into view, a syringe in hand. Virginia tried to pull away, but the straps held. The nurse sunk the needle into her arm and pushed the plunger down. Virginia's struggle lightened and a moment later, only her lips moved. Whatever was about to happen, they wanted her sedated, unable to resist.

I noticed a black x marked on the side of her temple. The spot pressed inward as the skin tore away and blood oozed down her head. The doctor materialized, a drill in his hand. He cranked it slowly, attempting to be precise. I had never heard the word before arriving here. A lobotomy. A procedure that pacified the most active patient. Fear of having a drill bore its way through your skull made everybody behave.

While the doctor's face remained hidden by a white mask, his eyes relayed his enthusiasm. When the instrument found its way into the skull, I could see the smile form beneath his rosy cheeks. He thrust the drill into the hands of an unseen assistant. Quickly he grabbed a thin metal spike.

Virginia's eyes fluttered, somewhere between sleep and consciousness. They relaxed as the instrument slid into the hole in her temple. With a careful twist, he pulled the tool out and admired his handiwork. Bits of brain clung to the spike, and I felt my stomach threaten to empty its contents on the floor. Like the visions before, I understood I had witnessed the hand of death. Except this time, the reaper took on the form of a mad scientist.

"Go to sleep," Virginia hissed.

I stumbled back, the piece of paper torn from her fingers as I landed on my backside. The light from outside bordered on blinding. I gasped for air, realizing I had stood watch as Virginia met God. The woman pulled the blanket over her face and turned away. I reached out, tempted to grab her shoulder and tell her to run. But I refrained. They could not cheat death.

Chapter Twenty-One

1942

"Child, you started and ended a war in a single night."

Claudette slapped the newspaper down on the table in the middle of her shop. The headline, "Mobster Midnight Massacre," rested above the fold, above the war. New York City had found itself victimized, the criminal underworld taking place front and center. I hoped every shop owner read the article with a sigh of relief.

"I can't take all the credit."

"According to this, they're blaming it on a rival gang."

I did nothing to hide the eye roll. We had left long before the cops arrived. I didn't expect any of the credit, but they could have attempted to be more accurate in their reporting. There was no evidence of another gang. But I understood. How could so many men with guns be killed without an army?

"You want credit for your deeds?"

I shook my head. "No, not credit. But I want the truth. I want them to explain how Bertolucci attempted to squeeze the citizens of New York. I want them to explain why half of the men killed were cops. I want real investigative reporting. This looks more like a tidy cover-up."

"Perhaps it is."

Claudette loved to drop hints at the bigger picture. She waited until I took the bait. "How do you mean?"

She folded the paper, setting it to the side of the table. Grinding herbs in the mortar, she prepared to slather half my body in the herbal remedy. I ached—no—I hurt. I could use her healing touch. She would need far more than this for the bruises I sported this morning.

"There is talk of another gang in town. Only whispers. Nobody seems to know anything about them. But after the men with the tattoos waged war, it does look like somebody is moving in on Bertolucci's territory."

I was about to object, but I found myself without a defense. Without the mob boss manipulating the city, did it leave a vacuum? Had I arranged for another to come in and put the same stranglehold on New York?

"You have the right idea, child. I'm not saying you were wrong in your mission. But maybe it's far from over."

I had anticipated this. Even without the ability to see the future, I knew the Society would demand my attention once the mob was gone. I had hoped they'd show last night, jump into the brawl so I could finally learn who pulled their strings. Had they sat back and watched from afar as I did their work for them?

"Do you think they wanted this?" I asked.

I had a hundred conspiracy theories about the Society, but so far no facts. Claudette could speak with the Lao, spirits connected to some other world. Perhaps they knew something.

"Their whispers are not for me. But they sense a great disturbance. What that is, I cannot tell."

Her spirits were more fussy than my ghosts. At least I could depend on mine to show me the future. Hers withheld more information than they gave. For a woman without gifts, she certainly knew a little about a lot.

"Take off your shirt," she held the bowl filled with the salve. The bruises had colored, a smattering of blue and purple painting my body. She started with my face. While many of the items in her shop had a delightful scent to them, the concoction used to reduce the swelling and hide my bruises bordered on putrid.

"It smells awful."

"Hush, child. Would you prefer people believing you get slapped about at home?"

I frowned like a petulant child. "No."

"Speaking of home," the toothy grin revealed the slight gap between her two front teeth. She knew something she shouldn't, "tell me about your engagement."

Damn angels.

"I see."

"I see? Really? That's all you have for me?"

Frank's face soured. The man had two emotions, stern and stern. I could never tell if things were bad from his facial expression. I elicited a frown from him more often than not. But being short with me, that was a sure sign he wasn't thrilled.

"What do you want me to say? We almost died last night."

"True," I said. "But we didn't. So can we focus on the positive?"

He stared at the paper on his desk. The photograph on the front showed a series of police chalk outlines from inside the warehouse. One of them belonged to Bertolucci. I wish it had a label, "Dead Mob Kingpin." I wanted the world to know he wouldn't be able to torment them any longer.

"So that's Edward."

"Subtle, Frank. Change the subject."

"What do you want, 'Nore? I'm concerned."

"They're dead," I said, pointing at the paper.

"Not about them. I'm concerned about you. You realize that you went head-first into the snake pit? You assumed you could take them on by yourself. If I hadn't been there, would you have died? If Edward hadn't arrived, would I have died? Have you thought about any of that?"

"I know when I die."

"Good. And me?"

He had always said he didn't want to know. I had avoided thinking about his death. Knowing his death meant it would cut the time spent with him short, no matter how long he survived. With a touch, the visions would lay it out bare for me. It seemed to be the only thing they eagerly revealed.

"Do you want to know?"

"We both know the answer to that." Frank wanted to live his life without an impending expiration date. While I remained partially submerged in the future, Frank felt it important to be rooted in the now. When I drifted to a world of probabilities, he anchored me.

"I was keeping an eye on you last night." Mostly a truth. Mostly.

"Eleanor, I say this with love. But you're not nearly as omnipotent as you've been acting. Sure, help make the streets safer. There's a line and you're crossing it. A mugger is a much different situation. This is dozens of killers. They're organized."

"They're gone." I couldn't fathom why he insisted on talking about the dangers that never came to fruition. The man seemed fixated on the past. The past meant nothing to me. I preferred to keep facing forward, to see the world as it could be, not what it was.

"You're not willing to talk about it. I get it." He leaned forward, elbows on the desk. He folded his hands together. "But you're being reckless. Seeing the future doesn't mean you're the master of it. You can't manipulate everything and expect it to turn out alright."

Not yet.

We sat in silence. The seconds passed, and we found ourselves in a stalemate. In my teen years, we ate dinner in silence. Our fights were legendary. I had believed Frank simply didn't understand. Layered underneath the anger was a world of hurt and remorse. If I looked backward, if I opened that door, I couldn't be sure I'd survive the heartache.

Susan Lee knocked at the door. She eased it open, holding a white box in her hand. "Sorry to disturb, but a courier just delivered this. It seems your man is in excellent form today."

She set the box in front of me. Hesitating, I knew Susan Lee wanted to see what it contained. She let out a sigh as she left. I knew the maneuver well, she'd chew through me later.

I pulled at the ribbon and flipped open the top of the box. Inside there was a neatly folded dress. Edward, in his fiancé duties, had stepped up his gift giving. I lifted the note on top of the garment. There was an address and time and a line promising no men in bomber jackets. I almost chuckled, almost.

"So Edward." Frank offered a truce, a conversation we could discuss. With two words, he waved the white flag. I was indeed lucky that the man considered himself my father.

"That's him. All the good and the bad rolled into one."

"He loves you."

I nodded. Frank had listened to me rattle on about the man like a young schoolgirl. I had made sure to keep the two of them apart for a long list of reasons. I didn't want Frank to judge my choice of boyfriend or have him accuse me of dating him just because we were both mentalists. But also, I didn't want Frank exposed to Edward. I could ward off his mental intrusions, but Frank didn't have that luxury. Edward best respect Frank's privacy and keep himself from rummaging around in his head. At this point, I had no way of knowing.

"He does."

"So," Frank let the word hang in the air.

"What are you getting at Frank? You're killing me here."

"What's it like being around another mentalist?" Frank knew about the three people in my life with gifts. I had made sure that Frank remained the single person who had all the facts about me. He preached honesty at his meetings. It was the least I could do.

"It's different." Frank raised an eyebrow. "He can sense things about me without needing to ask. He can't read my thoughts, but he can tell when I'm angry or when I'm in a particular mood. It was unsettling at first."

"He's your first."

I didn't particularly like the weight of that statement, but I let it slide. "We can speak volumes without moving our lips. Last night we took a tour of the Met. We never left his apartment, but there we were, surrounded by paintings." Frank did not need to know what we were doing on our cultural outing.

"Do you love him?"

Was the question complicated or did he want a simple yes or no? I nodded. "I think so, yes. He infuriates me, but he accepts me as I am."

"Do you accept him?" Frank smiled at the question.

"I think we know I'm difficult."

"Smart answer," he said.

"I asked him to marry me last night."

Would he refute my words? I prepared for the dropped jaw. But Frank simply nodded. It was not the behavior I had become comfortable with.

"We both know there's no talking you out of a decision. So all I can say is I wish you the best."

Frank knew and accepted me. "Thank you."

Frank fidgeted with the ring on his finger. I knew he had been married, but I never met his wife. When he first brought me to his home, there was only a single photo of the woman next to the couch where he slept. Frank never offered information about her. Even as a petulant child, I knew some ghosts deserved their rest.

"Nicole," he said softly, "her name, that is. She was," he took a deep breath. "Nicole was a wonderful woman."

"Nicole? That's the first time you've spoken her name."

"Your dad met her once when we were being deployed. He said, 'Frank, you're the luckiest bastard alive.' Your dad wasn't wrong. She had this outlook on life that defied logic. Bad things just needed to be polished to find the good."

"I wish I had met her."

"She would have hated you," Frank laughed. The man roared as he slapped the table. I didn't know if I should be offended or join in. "The two women in my life, so much alike, you'd have been a force together. She was pleasant, but cross her, and she had a temper that left me sleeping on the couch. She believed it built character and often said I needed more character."

"I'm not that bad, am I?"

"Imagine if Susan Lee had a temper."

"Oh." Susan Lee might very well be the most pleasant person on Earth. But I had seen her determination. If that joy turned to anger, not even Hell would stop her. "I guess you are the luckiest bastard in the world."

"I was." He eyed the ring. "I am. When I got back from duty, my first job was to speak to the spouses. Your mother was the hardest."

"I remember."

"You weren't—" His eyes widened. "You shouldn't have learned of his passing from me."

"I hated you before I knew you." I could recall him speaking softly with my mother. The memory was neither mine nor a memory. A vision had revealed the troublesome news. I watched it unfold. The day after, when I tried to tell Momma, she had slapped me across the face.

"The day after I started my vow of silence."

"Nicole is the reason I went back. She died of consumption. She wasted away until one day I had to bury my wife."

I sat quietly. I wanted to reach across the table and hold his hand. More than that, I wanted to wrap my arms around the large man and hold him. We started this conversation with an argument, and now he opened up about the only other woman in his life.

"I started drinking. I drank so much I'd blackout. But one night, I saw her. Can you believe that? Even in death, she turned around a bad thing."

"I see the future. My boyfriend can read thoughts. I believe it without question, Frank."

He ignored the sarcasm. The man wanted to believe his wife visited him in his hour of need. "I woke up and the only word that came to mind was family. I had no family, and your grandparents died long ago." My heart ached for the man. In the same breath, he bared a troubled heart and reminded me I wasn't alone.

"Frank…" I reached for him.

"I came back looking for you. And here we are."

I rushed around the desk, wrapping my arms around his neck. I wasn't quite sure what to say, a rare occurrence. Instead, I opted for silence, savoring the tender moment. I squeezed until he patted me on the arm.

"She'd want you to have this." I pulled my head from his neck and saw him holding the ring in his hand. He took my hand, placing it in my palm and closing my fingers. "I would make some idle threat about whooping Edward's backside if he does you wrong. But let's be honest, I'm out of my league."

"Frank…"

"Besides," he laughed. "I'm pretty sure you're more than capable of kicking his ass."

Nicole. I might not be the best person at remembering to smile through hardships. From a young age, I had my optimism beaten down until only anger and disdain remained. Staring at the thin gold band, I tried to think about the good in the future.

"Thanks, Pops."

Chapter Twenty-Two

1942

I had heard of salons before, where the elite gathered to discuss philosophy and immerse themselves in the finer elements of life, but I never expected to attend one. After hearing the word gala tossed around, I half expected a room full of smiling killers waiting to pounce. I felt foolish with a knife in my clutch. Almost.

Men and women waited at the door, their names being checked off a list. I found myself captivated by the mix of patrons. Not all who waited were dressed in finely tailored garments. Many had bits of paint visible for those willing to look close enough. I nearly cheered at the diversity, thankful to see New York's wealthiest willing to interact with laymen.

A gentleman escorting his wife took a slight bow, inviting me to step in line before them. I gave a slight courtesy. My ankle wobbled in the heels and I stumbled. My feet longed for the flat soles of my everyday boots. I cut in line and the gentleman at the door waited silently.

"Your name, dear," the man behind me said.

"Oh, thank you. Eleanor Bouvier."

The man at the door scanned through the list. He scanned it a second time, and I feared Edward intended to influence his way inside.

"I'm sorry, but I—"

"Try Eleanor Valentine," I said. "My fiancé might be overly enthusiastic about our engagement."

"It appears he is." The man smiled as he stepped to the side, giving me a slight bow. "Congratulations on the future, Mrs. Valentine." Even hearing him say the name made me smile. Perhaps forsaking my name and taking Edward's wouldn't be as demeaning as I first feared. However, I refused to be known as Mrs. Edward Valentine. I would allow none of that foolishness in my presence.

Piano music penetrated the low rumble of guests speaking. I jumped as a man stepped in front of me, a glass of champagne held in the center of a silver tray. I took the flute with a slight nod. Where the previous gala had been stuffy, this crowd felt alive, almost electric in their glee. I wasn't sure how Edward managed an invitation, but I found myself pleased with the man. I could learn to appreciate this side of Edward.

With him nowhere to be found, I thought it best to blend in. The works of art on the walls were exquisite. Without a creative bone in my body, I found myself in awe of the work. There were canvases appearing sloppily painted, and those that looked as if they were a photograph blown up life-size.

I listened to the men and women speak of the work, using words I had never heard. I consider myself an intelligent woman, but I quickly learned that being taught how to box and survive the streets to be a different kind of smart. But like me, the guests complimented and revered the artists. While I feared New York's wealthy might only be in attendance to brag about their latest acquisitions, they surprised me.

I could never tell what was good and what was not, but it left me feeling hopeful. That was until I stood in front of a canvas on the wall set inside an ornate gold frame. Isolated and avoided by the crowds, I found myself ensnared by the most heartbreaking scene suspended in the gallery.

Inside a diner, a man and a woman sat close enough to touch, their fingers only separated by the thinnest of spaces. A third man sat across the diner, an observer. Even the man behind the counter stared into space, distant, almost unaware of those in his establishment. A shiver ran down my spine, a kinship with the patrons in the diner.

"Dear, what is it you see?" asked a woman with a husky voice.

The woman had entered her twilight years. The hair hanging just above her forehead more gray than brown, and the wrinkles at the edge of her eyes and lips were plentiful. She had a beautiful smile and a demeanor that made me wonder if she might have grandkids. A quick glance and I saw we were alone in our corner of the gallery.

"I fear, I don't understand the question, ma'am."

"Josephine, but everybody calls me Jo." She turned back to the painting and for a moment we stood in silence. Much like the patrons of the diner, she was close enough to touch, but a distance remained. The loneliness was like an old friend, a drinking buddy who insisted on one more whiskey before hitting the road. I had watched the sunrise many nights in the company of loneliness.

"What is it you see as you admire this painting?"

"A diner. A man and woman—"

"No." Her statement cut me off. "Deeper, what do you *see*?" she asked as if the inflection in her voice might elicit a different response.

"I see—"

"No." I recalled a similar conversation with Edward when he taught me to conjure the imaginary flame.

"Loneliness." I took a slight step closer, peering into the tiny strokes making the woman's face. "There is a sense of sadness, sorrow even. He sits beside her, a boyfriend, maybe her husband? But there is an unsaid tension between them. She wants desperately to reach out, to bridge the distance and reunite with this man. But," I found tears starting to gather in the corner of my eyes. I reached into my clutch and produced a handkerchief. Dabbing my eyes, I steadied my breathing. "She is alone."

"I couldn't have put it more eloquently."

"Are you the artist?" I feared I had perhaps interpreted her work incorrectly or worse, made a fool of myself. "I apologize, I didn't mean—"

"My husband is the artist. I am but his muse."

I hadn't seen it before, but there was indeed a resemblance between the woman in the painting and my newfound companion. Had she been thirty years younger, it would have been uncanny. "He takes great care when he paints you."

The vision struck me quickly. The painting hung in front of Josephine and a gentleman. I assumed it was her husband shaking another man's hand, perhaps from the sale of this painting. It stood in its gold frame in a dozen different galleries. I gasped as I witnessed the life of a painting far into the future. The ceiling collapsed around it and manlike machines stormed the gallery, threatening to destroy the art.

The vision persisted. Jo's painting stood in a freshly painted room. Art hung on many of the surrounding walls, but only the one in front of me remained the same. I saw a man my age and next to him, an older gentleman. They hugged one another, a soft embrace as the younger man cried. I felt myself a voyeur in this private moment. Despite the sense of loneliness radiating from the painting, these two men closed the divide. They comforted one another in a way that warmed my heart.

I had never seen the gallery where this took place, but it must be one of the larger cities to be so spacious. High on the wall, behind where one man patted the back of the other, I could faintly make out a giant circular shape. It appeared as if it had the

head of a hawk and the body wrapped about. I did not understand what the vision wanted me to see, but something about the
painting struck me, a new perspective.

I spoke the words aloud in both my vision and the gala. "He's
reminding us to reach out, that we are only an arm's length from
those we need. We do not need to be alone."

"Dear, that gives me hope." Jo's voice pulled me from my
vision until I stood in the present. "Maybe one of these days he
will be brazen enough to sell this thing."

"Not him," I said, unsure of how to interpret the vision. "You.
We cannot wait on the idle whims of men. And when historians
look back, they'll remember that without you, this painting—"

"Nighthawks."

"Yes, Nighthawks," I knew this would not be the last I would
hear of this work of art, "it would collect dust without you."

"A woman after my own heart," she said, squeezing my hand.
"Never let that fire diminish, dear."

A hush passed through the gallery. All eyes focused on the
entrance.

"You have gathered tonight to admire art, drink wine, and put
thoughts of the war off until tomorrow." I nearly scoffed out
loud. It appeared even the enlightened elite still put the lap of
luxury before the horrifying realities taking place overseas. I
wondered how many men were draft dodgers, or how many
found ways to keep their sons from serving. The enchantment of
the evening faltered with a single line.

"It is with great pleasure that I invite you to mingle with our
guests from London. Having just arrived, I wanted to waste no
time introducing these visionaries."

The crowd clapped quietly, waiting for the first gander of the
people important enough to require an introduction. The
gentleman speaking took a bow and backed away from the door.
Tension in the air reached a fevered pitch.

"Oh no," I gasped.

Chapter Twenty-Three

1942

"Gregory," I whispered.

The man wore his signature gray suit, bits of color showing from the plaids in his tartan colored vest. My presence came as no surprise. Amidst the dozens of other women, he immediately locked eyes with me. A master of emotion, I couldn't tell if he was pleased or dismayed by my attendance.

Two women followed him into the foyer, both in elegant black gowns. One woman sported flowing red hair while her companion contained her golden hair in a tight bun with a single strand flowing down her face. Neither of them sported the American trend of pinned curls, a giveaway they came from a faraway land.

Gregory might have unsettled me, but it was Edward entering that shocked me. Did he know the women? Had he and Gregory exchanged words? I took great care to keep facets of my life separated, tucked away in their tidy compartments. These intertwined acquaintances had me worried.

Edward slid by, walking past the rush of patrons to greet the newcomers. He held out his hands, wrapping his arms about my waist. I kissed him on the cheek, my eyes still fixated on Gregory.

"I wasn't sure you'd come. We don't have a great track record when it comes to these things."

I pulled back, focusing on Edward. "No," I forced a smile, "we do not." Much to Edward's enthusiasm, this event wasn't shaping up to be any better.

I am honored that you decided to attend.

The words were soft, gentle even. I rested my hand on Edward's face, inspecting his eyes. It wasn't a man's thoughts pushing their way into my mind.

"You've been keeping secrets," I said.

At my request, Eleanor.

"Before you get flustered—" he started.

"Edward," I said with a low tone. "Are they—Is this the Society?"

"Yes," he said quickly. He put his hands on my face, forcing me to stare at his face. "But before you try to kill them, hear the full story. They're not at all what we expected. I promise, Eleanor, they're not the boogeymen we believed."

"They killed Bertolucci's men," I whispered.

"They weren't the only ones to take extreme measures."

He had a point. The Society had used men bearing the wavy lines as cannon fodder. We might have different approaches, but we had wanted to achieve the same goal. As I looked over his shoulder at Gregory bowing to a trio of female socialites, I swallowed my hypocrisy. We had been keeping the same secret, for very different reasons.

"I won't kill them."

Edward frowned. "Is that the best I'm going to get this evening?"

"I won't kill them if the telepath stays out of my head."

I can agree to these terms. For this evening, consider us hospitable guests. Please do enjoy yourself.

"See," Edward said.

I had never seen Edward broadcast his thoughts to multiple people. I noted the trick. He could influence more than one, so it should be safe to assume he could speak with multiple people. The evening transformed from admiring artwork to studying the opposition. I made sure the thought hung in my head, hoping the owner listened.

I imagined the flame in my mind. Growing from the dark, cement walls molded themselves about the fire. It vanished as I sealed the top of my barriers. This might lock away my abilities, but I knew the tactic made it nearly impossible for Edward to whisper in my head. I could only hope the visual prevented the woman from reaching into my head.

"I understand," he said with a kiss. Edward sensed that I safeguarded my mind. I returned the kiss, trying to make the best of this ambush.

"Who might be this be?"

Jo held out her hand. Without missing a beat, Edward turned, taking her hand and bestowing a gentle kiss on her knuckles. I wanted to be angry at the man for surprising me, but then he went and acted the perfect gentleman. I had conflicting emotions.

"Josephine, this is my fiancé, Edward Valentine."

"My husband is also named Edward. That can only mean trouble."

"With such beautiful women? Of course we'd be trouble."

"He is quite the charmer, isn't he?" She didn't quite sound convinced.

I had to admit, she was correct. "For all the aggravating things he does, he does make an effort."

Edward smirked. He knew how to wield his charm like a weapon. If I didn't know better, I'd claim that was his actual ability.

"Men," she chided, "they're all alike. One moment they're driving you mad, and the next they're begging for forgiveness."

She gave him a quick once over. "Eleanor, for a man this handsome, I might make an exception."

"If I wasn't betrothed to this wonderful woman, I'd gladly accept your exception."

Josephine raised an eyebrow at the overt compliment. She didn't hide the color rising in her cheeks or the surprise in her brow. "You must have done something incredibly wrong to be this charming."

"Ha!" I laughed. I hardly knew this woman, and already I wanted to call her my best friend. She had Edward reeling, struggling to speak his way out of the predicament.

"I must find my own Edward. I need to introduce him to a gentleman from the Chicago Museum of Art. He was speaking about my husband's painting. This may very well be the break he needs."

"If it weren't for women, these men would be nothing more than well-dressed animals."

"Eleanor, you only speak the truth," Josephine said with a slight curtsey.

As she vanished into the crowd of New Yorkers, Edward liberated two glasses of champagne. He handed me one of the flutes. Reaching up, he brushed a bit of hair behind my ear. For a moment, the rest of the crowd vanished, and only he and I existed. I thought of the painting, suddenly craving that connection to another human. I leaned my cheek against his hand, placing my hand over his.

"I love you," I said, raising my glass.

"To the future," he said, tapping his glass against mine.

"To our future." He sipped while I emptied the contents. His eyes widened as I finished the glass.

"Shall I find you another?"

"You knew what you were getting when you accepted my proposal." I held up my empty flute, shaking it to emphasize the lack of champagne.

"Yes, dear."

I nodded quickly. "I'm going to need more alcohol before the evening ends."

The Society. I avoided them like the plague. Never had I worked so hard at participating in trivial conversation. The Edward I first met had vanished. The ruffian had been swallowed by this dashing gentleman. He stood close to one of the women, idly chatting as they exchanged words with some painters. I cautiously watched, trying to get a grasp on their association. He almost appeared to have stepped from his pedestal to mingle with the humans.

"I heard they fled London before the war started," a woman gossiped. I stood with a trio of older women, trying to fit in. Sipping my champagne, I was no longer capable of counting how many glasses I had emptied.

Another of the women whispered. "Really? I heard they paid their way onto a ship and sailed here."

"They do have money," the first woman said.

"Oil you think? Perhaps their money is from land?"

I couldn't stand the speculation. The evening of intellectual conversation devolved into mind-numbing gossip. None of these women had the slightest clue where the trio came from. Their insistence on knowing facts to sound smart reminded me why I stayed in my part of the city.

I found Josephine entertaining a gentleman from the museum. Her husband appeared elated and I could only assume she brokered a deal for his artwork. I decided if I was going to be an outsider in a room full of people, I'd return to the painting that mirrored my own feelings.

Now that I had seen her husband, I could see that Josephine's Edward used himself as a model in the painting. It brought up more questions than it answered. Did this man have the same feelings of isolation that he depicted? Or did he simply put on display the underlying sentiment of New York City?

"It is an exquisite painting, is it not?"

I recognized the voice despite hearing it with my ears for the first time. I didn't turn to introduce myself. If she knew Edward, she already knew my name.

"A telepath."

"It seems there are more of us than I could have possibly imagined." In my peripheral, I could see her take a sip of wine. I gripped my clutch, holding it tight in case I needed to reach in for the knife.

"There would be more if they hadn't been slaughtered." I made sure my tone held a layer of accusation.

"Yes," she said. Her voice held no emotion. "It is a tragedy. We could have been something great."

I couldn't be sure, but it appeared the woman wanted to play a game of wits. The coy nature in which she spoke suggested she knew more information, but withheld it. If I continued asking questions, I'd show my hand. I had gambled enough to know a poker face when I saw one.

"Had I known, I could have stopped the killers sooner." Did she already know about my involvement? Did she know I pieced together that the killers worked for the doctor and his wife? Did they answer to the woman standing at my side? I had questions, but I swallowed them, waiting for her to speak.

"We appreciate what you did. The Society's expansion into America has started far more rocky than any of us could foresee. Boston is a lost cause, but New York City, she has promise."

"Are you going to claim they went rogue?"

"I am." Her statement held the same lack of emotion as before. Telepath or not, I believe I had found the woman's tell. Did she rely so heavily on her abilities that she lacked the simple ability to speak candidly with words?

"For a telepath, you seem to know little about those who work for you. Shame."

Yes, I insulted her outright. The game of information required jabs, well-placed tests to see how they defended. Once the weakness had been exposed, then you landed the hardest punch possible. I needed to see how she played this game before I attempted a final uppercut.

"Eleanor, you can't possibly understand the magnitude of the Society."

Deflection. A gentle parry. "From what I gather so far. They have infiltrated New York's elite and are using them to do their bidding. But it seems like you can't handle this expansion."

"Centuries ago, in London, the Paranormal Research Society was founded with a singular purpose. Men discovered a supernatural world, one with individuals who could influence the world around them with nothing more than their thoughts."

"Mentalists," I said.

She nodded. "At the center of this organization, there have always been four. Sought from across the globe, the Society collected our kind."

"But only four?"

"They fear us, Eleanor." The woman had an icy demeanor. "They treated us as test subjects. These scholars, the finest mankind had to offer, wanted to treat us as lab rats. They wanted to see the world through our eyes. They loosely disguised it as research, but truth be told, we were nothing more than animals for them to study."

"Were?"

"We are no longer their subjects. An entire organization built around mentalists should not remain in the hands of the captors."

"The animals control the zoo," I added.

"Crudely put." The woman thought of herself above me. I could hear the superiority coating her words like a fine powder.

Edward had a similar tone when he spoke of humans. I feared they were more similar than different.

"You say crude, I say honest. I find people who need to hide behind clever words to mask their insecurities. So now I wonder, what are you hiding?"

The woman turned to stare. The red hair spilling about her shoulders made her skin appear alabaster white. Coupled with the black dress, her skin looked positively radiant. She knew how to exude confidence in every aspect. But I knew she had never met somebody like me.

It took a moment before I realized the hum of conversation had stopped. Half the patrons had called it a night, leaving for their homes. But the silence turned quite unsettling when I realized the remaining guests had frozen still. I had seen Edward influence multiple people, but I suspected his abilities were far more limiting than this. Was I wrong? Could Edward control the minds of so many individuals?

"We are getting off on the wrong foot." Her smile held a less genuine joy and more the delight of a predator stalking its prey. "I am Olivia Sincerbeaux, telepath, one of the four in charge of the Society."

I expected the woman to hold out her hand and wait for me to kiss her rings. Her eye twitched slightly and her jawline showed as she clenched her teeth together. Edward had done the same thing before. She had reached her limit and taxed herself to control this many people.

"Eleanor Bouvier, telepath, New York City's protector."

I tried to hide the threat, but I wanted her to know I'd stand against her if forced. I had no idea the abilities of her female companion, but if necessary I could have a knife against Olivia's throat. A woman so obsessed with demeanor most likely hadn't spent enough time in the ring to stop me.

"You are a curious creature."

"You said four. It appears you're missing one of your mentalists."

"A coup is not without its losses. Our dear Robert fell victim to those unwilling to relent their power." Did she just threaten me? While knowing Edward and Claudette gave me a sense of belonging, a clan bigger than myself, Olivia's presence lacked comfort. The woman left a sour taste in my mouth.

"They tasked the doctor and his wife with finding mentalists. We are no longer beholden to our captors. A Society composed of mentalists could be a powerful force. With our resources, we could find a suitable position in the world. Unfortunately, they held onto the belief that mentalists should be feared. We seek to strengthen our ranks, they sought to diminish them."

"Seven, they killed seven mentalists."

"But we found a fourth to complete our council." She glanced over my shoulder. The hair on my arms stood on end as I realized there was only one man she could mean. I'd feared Edward might someday have aspirations, but I never imagined they'd be with an organization that housed killers.

"To what end?"

"Eleanor," she said my name as a mother says to a child. I suddenly realized that Olivia thought of me as nothing more than a juvenile mentalist. Under any other circumstance, I'd show her a fierce right hook, but for now, I wanted to maintain my inferior telepathic abilities. A proper feign on my behalf could result in a match-ending blow later.

"Can you imagine a world where there is no deceit? No secrets? We have gifts that could benefit all of mankind."

"War?"

"You think us selfish? Perhaps our role is to make sure a war like this never occurs? What if we have the ability to build something that sees that no war erupts ever again? Imagine your nightly jaunts into the city, but across the globe."

Her words had merit. Alone, I thwarted a mugger, a robber, even a band of mobsters. With their combined resources at my back, we'd be able to stop crime without a fight. With a simple command... I imagined a world where a single entity controlled the destiny of a species. The line formed a barrier I dared not cross.

Just this morning Frank attempted to pull me back from that division between right and wrong. My father feared a future where my selfish behavior caused harm, or worse. Frank feared the moment I crossed over to believing I was more, better, and greater than. I whispered his warning, "We are not nearly as omnipotent as we believe."

"Don't mumble, dear." I contemplated dropping the walls, exposing my flame. Drawing the energy from the room, from Olivia, I might be capable of summoning a vision. A glimpse into the future might show me how to best proceed.

I flexed my fingers, ready to figuratively strike the woman. In a room filled with stationary people, a cool breeze flowed along my arms. The tension in my hands eased, and I released a breath slowly. I had experienced the tingle in my chest many times over the last month. Gregory's gifts, even with my mind walled off, still had the ability to penetrate my defenses and manipulate my emotions. The man siphoned away my aggression, robbing me of my anger, and replaced it with a soothing calm.

In all our meetings on the park bench, he only demonstrated the mastery of his gift to provide clarity. I didn't know if I could trust him. But for a moment, I believed he understood what made me tick enough to know I was about to do something rash. I hoped for Gregory's sake he held only good intentions.

"I said I'll consider the proposition."

Olivia smiled. Even through the calm, I wanted to rake my nails down the flawless skin of her face. But I had learned that bullies always led with their strongest hand. The leader of this organization wanted to land the opening blow. She had, by snaring Edward in her trap. But I was more than familiar with taking a punch. I'd win by focusing on the long game.

"This pleases me."

With that, the patrons resumed their conversation as if time hadn't passed. They continued about the room, saying their farewells as the event came to a close. I turned back to the painting. Olivia tried to impress me in a show of force, and already I conspired how I would put an end to this potential threat to my city.

"Eleanor, dear, let me introduce you to the others."

"Before you get mad—"

"Mad?" It was hard to be mad as we entered a hotel suite, unlike anything I had ever experienced before. The living room alone was bigger than my apartment, furnished with the latest decor. The opulence of the room provided a momentary distraction, but I had an uncanny ability to retain anger.

"I didn't—"

"Didn't what? Think it was worth mentioning you knew other mentalists? Or did you decide to hide that once you discovered they were part of the Society? Edward, do I need to remind you they almost got us killed?"

"Eleanor, you need—" He stopped himself short of telling me to calm myself. Right now I was just short of throwing glass lamps. The fact I hadn't drilled my knuckles into his jaw was as close to calm as I could muster.

"Edward, do you not see how she's manipulating the situation?"

"How do you mean?"

I plopped myself down on the couch, disturbed by how such a decadent piece of furniture managed to be so uncomfortable. I turned to see Edward apprehensive. He feared a knockdown fight erupting at any moment. At least that gave away a layer of guilt somewhere underneath the sheer stupidity.

"Sit."

He sat next to me, with just enough distance I couldn't easily slap him. Edward did indeed know me.

"They nearly had us killed. I'm not buying how the doctor went rogue. I'm not buying it for a second. Nobody with her abilities would allow a random couple to go rogue. And what of the men in the bomber jackets? Has she explained that?"

"In fact, she has." He pulled off his suit jacket, tossing it over the arm of the couch. "This is an old organization from another time. Only those with high social standing or deep pockets were allowed to join. But the Society had a price." He paused, and I could tell I wouldn't like the next sentence out of his mouth. "They had to sacrifice their firstborn."

"What the hell?"

"Didn't you say the doctor mentioned losing his son?"

I replayed the conversation in my head. The mother had somehow turned her child into that insane killer. I hadn't considered there was more than a single deranged woman and her killer child. But it did fall in line with what the doctor said. Perhaps he had remorse for their actions? Perhaps it had been the woman who clawed her way into an organization? Without Olivia spoon-feeding answers, I doubt I'd ever know for sure.

"Olivia and Robert created them. They are the price of admission, or at least they were. It's one of the things that she wants to do away with. Be as suspicious as you want, but she wants what's best."

"For who, Edward? Who does she want the best for? Her? Us? Who are we to play God? These gifts don't make us more than other humans. We can't right every wrong."

"Says the woman who puts on a mask to save New York City each night."

"That's different."

"No," he shook his head, "it's not, Eleanor. You keep saying that, but it's not. You are trying to do right by the city. But with Olivia, Catherine and Gregory, I can do right. We can change the face of the world. No more stopping muggers. We can stop crime. No more winning battles. We can stop war."

"By what? Robbing them of free will?"

The question hung in the air. It had always been a point of contempt between Edward and I. There was a difference between him influencing a waiter to bring a glass of wine and wiping out the free will of the people. Try as I might, I couldn't change his point of view. I had admitted long ago, I would either need to live with it, or end our relationship.

"So what if that is what she aims to do? I am being inducted as one of the four. This will give me the ability to sway their decisions. I can help make this a force for good."

The night before, I stood face to face with Bertolucci, a man who allowed power to corrupt his very soul. It twisted him until he was nothing more than a thug trying to hoard his status away from the world. I wanted to believe that Edward could resist the influence of Olivia and the Society, I really did. But I had seen him step over the line more than once.

I imagined that somewhere in Edward's chest, along the outside of his heart, a black spot had appeared. With the promise of power, wealth, and status, the Society had already infected the man I loved. We might not be perfect, but we were happy. I did not want to lose him to the darkness.

"I don't want to fight," he reached out, leaning closer so he could put my hands between his. He rubbed it gently, his face somewhere between worry and concern. "You don't know what the future holds. We can shape it together."

It was true, in this one regard, I didn't know what the future held. Despite the rage in the pit of my stomach that refused to subside, I wanted to be the one to wash away his dark spot, and shine a light for a heart with so much potential.

A painting hung on the wall between two massive windows. Unlike the works in the gallery, it had a generic feeling to it. Yellow flowers with blue stems waved in the wind, eliciting absolutely no emotion. The rest of the room had a similar feel, beautiful yes, but sterile in nature. But against the white backing of the couch, Edward tried his damndest to convey sincerity through his eyes.

"No promises when it comes to that woman or her intentions."

"I would expect nothing less of you."

"I will tear her down the moment I witness her step out of line."

"You wouldn't be you if you didn't."

Sweet talker. He knew exactly how to win me over. I opened my clutch, setting the knife on the coffee table. Edward made no comment. He knew me well enough. I would never have attended an event like this without a weapon of some sort. Unfortunately, brass knuckles are heavy and don't easily fit in a clutch.

"Edward Valentine," I pulled Frank's ring from the clutch. I held it up between us, his eyes fixated on the thin band of gold. "Our lives do not offer us the luxury of a wedding. Perhaps someday we will have a worthy celebration. But until then, consider this a vow."

"Eleanor Bouvier, first you propose, now this? I might almost get emotional."

"Don't make me punch you."

Edward held up his hand, bearing his ring finger for me. We were less than traditional in every regard. It only made sense we continued as such. I slid the ring over his finger, surprised that his fingers were almost as thick as Frank's paw.

"Edward, I promise to be your light. And together, we'll move mountains."

"Eleanor," he scooted closer, placing his forehead against

mine. "For some reason, fate saw it fit for us to meet. She is thankfully a benevolent mistress."

I kissed him gently, trying to believe that fate had provided me something good. I wanted her to offer me a break, a way to end the cycle of pain. Hopefully, this was a new chapter and that Edward would stand by my side.

"I'm still angry with you."

"I expect nothing less, Mrs. Valentine."

Chapter Twenty-Four

1942

The soft bed made it impossible to sleep. While Edward snored, lost in his dreams, I needed the quiet symphony of the city below. The hotel was far more expensive than anything I could afford, even with my illegal winnings. With Bertolucci gone, I would have to find an alternative source of income. It might be time to learn a skill and put it to use. I had never considered it, but perhaps I could contribute to the war effort by becoming one of the riveters?

I pulled on a bathrobe, tying the belt about my waist. Moving through the suit, I had to wonder how much money Olivia and her organization held. If the initiation required the sacrifice of their firstborn, did they also pass a collection plate? I loved Edward, but I worried he hadn't asked enough questions before agreeing to partake in this endeavor. But what if he had? What if he'd asked every question crossing my mind, and he found the risk acceptable? Neither question calmed my racing thoughts.

The windows were sealed shut, unable to open and let in the sounds of the city. I put my hand on the glass, hoping I'd be able to feel its pulse. This high above the city, all I could feel was cold glass. We were on the sixteenth floor, and I marveled at the city as it spread out in a vast network of buildings. I found myself uncomfortable with this view, this ability to look down on the people of New York. I wondered if Olivia did this intentionally, assuming her place was amongst the clouds with the gods?

The rug under my feet was deep enough that my toes lost themselves. Moving through the living room, I reached the double doors leading into the hallway. The brass fixtures stood out against the stark white of the paint. I pulled them open, revealing the short corridor. There were three similar suites on this floor, with Olivia down the hall opposite of us. I imagined she had long since gone to bed, satisfied that her plans were unfolding.

In one room, an empath slept, while across the hall roomed Catherine, a woman with the ability to manipulate objects with her mind. I did not understand the extent of her abilities, but in the next few days, I'd be sure to question her extensively. I understood Gregory's gifts, and how he weaponized them. It was Catherine who remained an oddity.

For months, the empath had been training me to utilize my abilities. I hadn't made significant breakthroughs, but I appreciated his tutelage. However, my fondness for the well-dressed foreigner had been undercut when I realized he was part of the same organization he warned me against. My guard had been lowered, and I feared he had taken advantage of me and my abilities. I needed to speak with him and unearth what information Olivia truly knew about me.

On one floor, there was an immense amount of potential. I understood Edward's desire to be involved. The same thing had drawn me to him, Claudette, and later Gregory. I didn't want to bear the burden of being alone, the only one who suffered through life with a secret. But that feeling of belonging didn't extend to Olivia. Something about the woman's actions tugged at my moral compass.

She explained every question, almost to the point where it felt rehearsed. Did the doctor and his wife really go rogue? Were they trying to prevent the Society from expanding their influence in America? I imagined they were distraught over the loss of their son, so it made for a plausible explanation.

But what about the men with the wavy marks on their wrists? The man who attended Frank's meeting must have wanted to maintain some semblance of his life. Did he drink because of the horrible things he would do? Then why go to the support group? He didn't strike me as a man who knew he'd be throwing away his life. After watching Olivia freeze an entire room of socialites, I had no doubt she could influence a man to undertake a suicide mission.

The elevator dinged.

The doors opened, and I nearly tripped over myself as I fell backward. Three men in bomber jackets stepped out. They moved in perfect harmony, even their steps acting in unison. I pushed back, trying to reach the couch. My knife remained on the coffee table and without the robe, I'd be more than capable of fighting them in my underwear.

The men never looked in my direction. I remained invisible as they gathered around Gregory's door. I screamed, trying to garner their attention. The man in the lead kicked at the door. I crawled to my hands and knees and up the back of the couch. My knife had been removed from the coffee table. I searched for my clutch, but to no avail.

The robe came off and I threw it to the floor. I didn't need a knife, I could manage dispatching the three killers. Through the hallway and into Gregory's room, I moved with haste. Instinctively, I reached behind my back and found my missing knife resting in the jacket holder.

"What..."

I patted my chest, suddenly aware I wore my jacket. My fingers were coated in the familiar charcoal. I decided to worry about my sudden transformation after I dispatched Gregory's assassins.

In the room, two of them barreled through the glass doors leading to Gregory's bedroom. I snuck behind the one who watched from the living room. With a harsh slash, the knife passed through the man's back. I thrust again, watching my hand swallowed by the killer's jacket. Reaching out with my free hand, I gasped as my fingers passed through the man's neck.

"It's not real."

Edward had often teleported us to locations across the city. I wondered if this was any different. Was he trapping me in this virtual mindscape? Perhaps Olivia? Were they showing me something, or was this my own doing? For a moment I contemplated barging into her hotel suite and holding her hostage until she released me.

I watched as the two men pinned Gregory to the bed. One dragged a blade across his neck while the other held a pillow firmly over his face. He struggled and thrashed on the bed despite a killing blow being dealt. It ended as his body grew still, then limp. Gregory, the man who had taught me to harness my powers, had been murdered in his sleep.

The two men who killed him returned to the living room. They were like the others, buzzed heads, bomber jackets, but more disturbing was seeing the trio of twisted smiles. The man in front of me spun around and the stretched lips were only inches from my face. I gasped as they stepped through me, making their way for the same elevator that had brought them here.

I watched as they stepped into the hallway, then the elevator. As the brass doors closed, I was left alone. I couldn't fathom that the man had died. Masterful in his abilities, surely he could have held them at bay. Perhaps he thrust out a wave of fear, terrifying the killers until they bolted. But no, the Gregory in this vision had died with little more than a thrashing.

"I'm sorry."

A morbid curiosity took over. I walked through the room, the knife still clenched in my right hand. I stood over the man's bed, looking at the growing stain of red. They left the pillow used to silence him on his face. For some reason, that bothered me. I wanted to see the man's face one last time. Reaching for the white fabric, my fingers harmlessly passed through.

"I'll find them," I promised. "I'll find them and kill them just like before."

The plush white blanket obscured the man's body. The red of his blood continuing to spread, soaking through the sheet and along the pillows. Part of me wanted to lash out, to rally, but as I stood there accepting the inevitable. I was reminded of Benjie. Helpless, I accepted the atrocity.

It was only a matter of time, but Gregory would die.

Chapter Twenty-Five

1931

I was scared to say goodbye.

The straps tightened around my wrist, securing me to the gurney. I struggled, trying to push back the two men holding me down. I raked my nails against an orderly with my free hand. He shouted obscenities as he covered his eye. I attempted to swipe again, but his partner lay across my chest, grabbing my arm. With my second wrist bound, I started swinging my legs.

"She's a real piece of work," the two-eyed orderly said.

"Fucking bitch is what she is." He pulled his hand back and snarled when he saw the blood streaking his hand. I tried to kick him, my knee almost reaching his stomach.

"Grab her legs," the other one said.

"You're going to wish it was just me and you. Now you need to see the doc." The three shimmering red gashes on his face only made his smile more sinister.

For a week they had locked me away in a separate wing of the hospital. Away from the other patients, I became nothing more than a memory—for those with a memory. The room had no windows. The only light came from the gap under the door. I'm sure I heard rats at night, or day. I couldn't be sure.

But it wasn't until the third time I fell asleep my eyes adjusted enough to see the grooves on the wall. I ran my hands over them, trying to memorize them with my fingertips. Rough and narrow, they seemed as if somebody had been chiseling away at the wall. I spent the rest of the evening crying as I discovered their origins. On the floor, a fingernail revealed the only clue I needed. I fought a battle in which neither side won. Live, due to sheer stubbornness, or will myself to die. Meanwhile, I hovered in limbo, waiting for somebody to decide my fate.

They tightened the straps around my ankles until I feared they'd cut the skin. I was trapped. The wheels on the gurney squeaked as they wheeled me down the hall. I didn't need to see my destination to know what awaited. I had seen the same thing happen to Virginia. It was my turn to vanish in the middle of the night.

One of the men raised the gate on the elevator while the other wheeled me in. We descended into the bowels of the hospital. No patient had seen what lay ahead and survived to speak of it. The ghosts had made sure I knew, one last effort for the demons to scare me. I almost laughed. The ghosts lost their ability to inspire fear.

"Bets on how long she lasts?"

"Hopefully not as long as the last one. It turns my stomach when they gurgle."

The elevator stopped and the gate lifted. The corridors no longer looked like halls. Rough stone and exposed dirty walls made it look as if we had descended into the earth. Hell.

We passed another gurney, a white cloth draped over the body underneath. I didn't need to look at the hair, I knew it was Virginia. Her body decayed beneath the same place that promised to make her better. Within the hour, they would line my body up behind her, left on display to torture the doctor's next unwilling victim.

"Wait here, heh," said one of the men as they both disappeared inside a nearby room.

They whispered, low enough that I couldn't hear. I recognized the voice of the doctor who oversaw the psychiatric ward. Three men discussed my fate, my inevitable demise. These men were more ghastly than the demons who haunted my childhood. The moment I realized they were the definition of evil, the ghosts didn't seem so bad. They haunted me, but they had never done me physical harm, nor had they slaughtered women in the pursuit of science.

I would not be complicit in my own demise.

The restraint whined as I pulled. I fought. The leather cut into my wrists, rubbing enough that I could feel the wetness of blood. I leaned hard, hoping I could slide my hand free. Like Virginia had, I thrashed violently, hoping for a different outcome. Just when the gurney threatened to tip, an orderly caught me. One grabbed the sides of my head while the other inserted blocks and tightened the strap over my forehead. I tried to resist, I tried so damned hard.

"It won't be long now," one of them whispered.

Minutes later, I was in the room and the doctor jabbed me in the arm with a needle. He made no small talk, no statement of what was to come. I had been written me off as an acceptable loss. He dehumanized the situation, pursuing discovery in the name of science with disregard for life.

I tried to fight, but my arms grew heavy as the doctor took a marker to my head, marking the incision location. My muscles refused to cooperate, and the thrashing reduced to mild twitching. The orderlies' faces vanished in a blur. No longer did evil men watch over me. They were replaced by faceless demons, fiends who prepared to watch me die so they could collect a paycheck.

For years I considered myself a coward, too scared to take my own life. I had thought of at least a dozen ways I might end my life. I lacked the courage or the conviction. But now, as the doctor offered me a solution, I found he was like the ghosts robbing me of choice. I did not want to die, not by his hand, not without choice.

The drill touched my temple.

Ghosts filled the room, ready to say their goodbyes.

A blur burst through the door. I could hardly make out the shape, a man, an enormous man. The scratched orderly screamed out but stopped after a loud thud. I watched as the flash of white fell to the floor. Another thud came from the floor, and I could only guess it resulted from a kick to the orderly.

The doctor pulled the drill away from my head, the tip no longer resting against my skin. I looked up, but couldn't see the man anymore. "Stop him. He'll ruin everything."

An orderly had his arms up like he might start boxing. The man jabbed, popping the orderly in the face. The man ducked a wide-sweeping hook, and the orderly jumped up as the man struck him in the torso. Whoever the man was, he had gotten into his fair share of skirmishes before. I didn't know who he was, but I rooted for him, praying he'd kill everybody in the room.

"What have you done?" It was a statement, not a question. The doctor cowered somewhere behind me, putting as much space between himself and the man. Something rattled and a metal tray fell to the floor. "Stay back. I'll defend myself."

"Ellie is coming with me." The voice didn't waver. The owner meant each word and nothing the doctor could do would get in the way. "You'll have to kill me before you hurt her."

The man had a square jaw, and for a moment I believed Poppa had come to my rescue. Even with the blurry vision, I could see the man's ghost as clear as day. It stepped forward, holding still for a moment, assessing the doctor. The clarity of the ghost reinforced my belief, I had no idea who the man in the room might be.

The ghost of an orderly popped into view, throwing his arms around my savior. I had wanted to die, to will away the pain of living. Being tied to the table made me realize that if I was going to die, it would be by my doing. In a split second, the world changed. I wanted to live.

"Behind you." I didn't recognize my voice.

The man spun about. The orderly held him in a bear hug. By sheer strength, he freed one of his arms and brought his elbow down on the man's shoulder. The orderly loosened his hold, and the man grabbed the back of his head, slamming his knee into the orderly's face. He slumped to the floor.

The doctor rushed the man, a long metal spike in his hand. I couldn't see their bodies as clearly as I could, the ghost acting a fraction of a second faster than their owner. I struggled against the straps, hoping I could free an arm or even a leg. Restraining patients appeared to be the only job the orderlies managed.

The doctor tried to shove the spike into the man's chest. I marveled at how quickly the man's arms moved. He grabbed the doctor's wrist with his left hand, punched inside the crook of the elbow with his right. The spike changed direction and with a shove, it vanished into the lab coat and pushed past the rib cage. Just like that, the doctor's future had been written. I didn't need the ghosts to tell me death hovered nearby, waiting to claim its victim.

"Ellie," it was almost difficult to hear him over the sputtering of the doctor. "Your father asked me to find you before he died."

"Poppa?" I couldn't hold it back. Tears pooled in my eyes as I sobbed. I hadn't been able to save my father. The ghosts showed me his death, but I couldn't change the future. However, from beyond the grave, my father saved me.

The man pulled at the strap across my forehead and then freed my arms. His coarse hands rested on my arms. Sitting me up, he hugged me in an awkward gesture. He held me tight for a moment before whispering in my ear. "He wanted me to remind you, it's his job to save you. Not the other way 'round."

I returned the hug, gripping the man tightly. The ghosts flooded the room, and I saw him removing the straps from my legs and carrying me from the basement. But there was another ghost, the doctor. He made it out alive, even if he didn't make it further than that.

I pushed the man away to see the doctor reaching for a scalpel on the floor.

"He..."

The man quickly kicked the weapon away. Lifting the doctor to his knees, the man grabbed his head. With a fierce turn, I heard the snapping bones in his neck. The doctor died. Not in the hallway where he should have, but in the room. The ghosts they had been right about his demise, but not how. As the man lifted me from the table, I had to wonder if I had been wrong about the future. Could it be molded?

I cradled my head against the man's chest. I didn't know his name, but I recognized him. He provided the same awkward hug to my mother the night he explained the tragedy. I never saw him with my own eyes, but I recognized him from the vision. Again his fate weaved into my life.

"I know you..." My eyes closed, and I stopped resisting the drugs.

"Frank," he said, "Everything is going to be better from now on."

Goodbye, but not the one I had imagined.

Chapter Twenty-Six

1942

Catherine stood at the foot of the bed. The blankets and sheets on the bed hovered in the air. Her own hair spread about her head as if it had a life of its own. I couldn't be sure, not from lying in the bed, but it appeared as if she, too, floated above the floor.

I was thankful I found one of the nightgowns in the hotel closet. Edward didn't have a shred of modesty, if anything he enjoyed having his naked self on display.

"Catherine? What are you doing here?"

The woman's face was red with rage. Her fingers balled into fists and I couldn't imagine how I might fight the woman if circumstances required. If she wanted, she could easily spin my head, snapping my neck. I'd have never even gotten out of bed.

"They killed him in his sleep."

I fought away the sleep. Rubbing my eyes, I sat up. I nudged Edward until he startled awake. He reached out, trying to draw me close so he could nuzzle my neck while we slept. The moment he realized the blankets were out of reach, he opened his eyes and then shot upright.

"What's going on?"

"Gregory," I didn't need to hear the phrase. I knew what had occurred. More than that, I had watched it unfold. "They killed him."

"What? No. What?" Edward couldn't process the information. "Who?"

I understood her anger in that moment. Somebody close to her, even if they weren't friendly, had been attacked. It was a violation. I bit my tongue, careful to not reveal my understanding of the situation. I hoped Catherine or Olivia could piece together who the killer might be.

"Barren. They killed Gregory last night."

"Barren?" I asked.

"The firstborns. One of them came here last night. They murdered him in his sleep."

Three actually, but I held off correcting her. The anger in her voice made me think more highly of her. I hardly knew the man outside of our sessions in the park, and my stomach was in knots. Last night I witnessed his death, and once the vision ended, I calmly returned to sleep. Had I known, I might have been able to force myself awake and save Gregory.

"How? Couldn't he stop them?"

She whipped the blanket and sheets against the far wall. Catherine fell to her knees, sobbing. Her crying unsettled me. I believed them to be more like work companions, distant, but working toward a common goal. For whatever reason, it hadn't crossed my mind that they may have actual affection for one another.

"The Barren have no emotions to manipulate."

I looked past the sobbing mentalist to see Olivia standing in the living room. The woman was already dressed. While not the over-the-top gown from the night before, she still managed to portray a woman with money. The dress hugged her hips, the hem cut at an angle that revealed one of her knees while the other hid behind the fabric.

"I don't understand."

"You, I, or Edward could control their empty minds. Catherine would have had no problem stopping them. Gregory, however, he can't read emotions that aren't there. He had no defense against those beasts."

Edward crawled off the bed, kneeling next to Catherine. He rubbed her back like a gentleman. I scooted to the end of the bed, crossing my legs while I tried to wrap my head around the situation.

"Eleanor," Olivia said, "we are at war."

"With who?"

"The Society has existed for hundreds of years. There are hundreds if not thousands of humans scattered across the globe. But there are only ever four mentalists. It appears they dislike mentalists, us, being liberated."

Catherine sobbed gently and Edward held her, Olivia was the polar opposite. Her cold and distant demeanor was far more terrifying than a woman capable of hurling me against a wall like the sheets.

"Can you find them?"

"They created the Barren to be the perfect killer. Even for a telepath as talented as myself, I can't reach out and find them."

"Do you have a list of members? Can we track them down?"

"There may have once been a list of members, but the record keeper was one of the men lost in London."

Killed, she meant killed. I tried to overlook the technicality. "Then how do you plan to stop them? Is there anything Edward or I can do?"

"You've had a change of heart?"

The image of Gregory resisting, trying to struggle free from the Barren would haunt me. I had a list of ghosts that occupied my head, struggling to break free from the boxes in which they were buried. I had taken to the streets to make them safer, and if I could avenge his death, it would be a step in the right direction.

"The devil you know," I said, letting her know I distrusted her.

"Not the acceptance I hoped for." Her tone returned to the superior woman from the night before. She believed the moment I accepted the offer, I'd fall in line behind her lead. The woman's ego rivaled the vilest of men, but again, I knew her. I couldn't allow mentalists to be slaughtered again. For now, I wanted her close.

"Trust is earned, Olivia. It's not granted to those who believe themselves superior. Remember that."

She gave a slight nod. "It might not be the acceptance I expected, but we have more pressing matters."

No, I did not trust the woman in the least.

"I'll prepare the initiation."

"The what?" What could be more important than the body soaking the sheets?

"There are rituals to be performed with his passing." I wanted to clock her.

"Somebody killed Gregory and you're worried about formalities?"

"It is who we are," she said, as if that answered every question.

And like that, her concern over Gregory vanished. If I wasn't already suspicious of the woman, her ability to push away tragedy would have raised red flags. She cared more about securing her position than she did those who fell in her pursuit of victory. For a moment, I had to wonder if Olivia's hands were red with blood. Did she have anything to do with the Barren targeting Gregory?

In my head I could only hear a single phrase, "There have always been four."

"I'll deal with it." Olivia's words had held an eerie quality. I couldn't fathom how one might dispose of a body. She hardly batted an eyelash at the situation. There was no question in my mind. They had done this before. Is this the world for mentalists or did money allow these situations swept under the rug?

The visions were coming more quickly. One by one, the people in my life who understood the meaning had been stolen. First Edward submitted himself to the Society, determined to hold one of the four positions, and without so much as a consideration for what it might mean. Then Gregory lay in a pool of his own blood. I had one confidant left and fear required I verify she remained untouched.

The gown brought more than one curious glance. My evening attire now looked like the mad ravings of a desperate woman. I didn't dare return to the apartment. I wanted Susan Lee to have no part in this disaster. As I stomped along the sidewalk, a woman walking arm-in-arm with her husband shot me a disgusted look. I nearly hurled an insult, but her ghost took me by surprise.

The swirl of emotions stirring deep in my belly made it difficult to maintain any level of focus. I unraveled. Thoughts of the Society sinking its hooks into Edward had me angry. The blank look on Gregory's face tugged at my heart. In a single night, my world had been jostled and turned upside down. I needed guidance, a guardian angel.

I turned into the alley off the main road leading to Claudette's herbal shop. I braced myself against a wall, taking a moment to breathe deeply. I pushed the conflicting emotions away and focused on my breath. Slowly in through the nose before letting the air slip out between my lips. I repeated the meditation technique, hoping it would allow some semblance of control. The imaginary flame stopped flickering and dimmed to the tiniest sputtering of orange and red.

"Claudette," I threw open the door to her shop. "Are you here?"

The empty shop caused my heart to race. No meditation would stop me from panicking if another person in my life died. I made my way to the counter when the door opened. Claudette stood in the doorway, attempting to read the situation. Her eyes focused on the dress. She knew something was amiss.

"Child, what's wrong?"

"Gregory, he's dead." There was so much more I wanted to blurt out, but it was the easiest one to explain.

"They're here," she said in a hushed tone.

I nodded.

"Have a seat, child. I'm going to bring you some tea. You need to relax. You have the spirits agitated. They're whispering faster than I can hear."

I took a seat at the large wooden table in the middle of the room. I looked at the jars of herbs and recognized enough of them to know she had been creating something to stop the pain. Drops of blood lined the edge of the table, speckling the wood. At some point this morning, or perhaps last night, she had dealt with a person in duress.

"Is everything okay?" I nodded to the drops of blood.

"A gunshot to the arm. He wailed like a banshee."

The mob had been decimated and all that remained were goons without a leader. It was part naivety and part wishful thinking, but with the Bertolucci gang gone, I expected crime to subside. There would always be those who preyed on the weak. Tonight, I'd go onto the streets and face a new opponent, but I wouldn't stop. I wanted to ask who shot the man, but I caught myself.

"It's none of your concern, child."

She set down a tray with cups and a metal tea kettle. Before pouring, she opened a glass jar, sprinkling in dry herbs. Adding tea, I breathed deep, inhaling the warm smell. Whatever she added to the bottom of the cup already calmed my mind and relaxed my muscles.

"Drink up. Then we can discuss what's happening."

Claudette pushed the cup toward me. As I took another whiff, she put her finger under the cup, forcing me to drink or spill it down my shirt. She continued raising her finger, and I gulped down the hot liquid. My throat was on fire, but with each swallow, the herbs took effect and I found myself leaving hysteria.

"That's amazing." I wiped my lips as I set the cup on the table.

Claudette poured herself a cup, not nearly as eager to empty the glass. She took a small sip and then rested against a stool, finally ready to listen. "Now, tell me what has gotten you worked up so."

The story had no start and end. I blathered incessantly and I'm sure I repeated details multiple times. I explained Olivia's take on the Society, Edward's involvement, and ultimately the death of Gregory. As I spoke about Olivia and Catherine, I mentioned their abilities. Claudette listened quietly, only raising an eyebrow when I mentioned Olivia freezing a room full of people. She knew when to nod her head and when to purse her lips with concern.

I reached the end, staring into the bottom of my empty teacup. As I held it out, she refilled it without saying a word. Patience had never been a virtue I possessed and waiting for her to respond to the wild tale had my skin crawling. Sipping the tea, I stared over the cup, hoping Claudette would break her silence.

"What do you make of it?"

That's it? After a tale of murder, secret organizations, and a boyfriend who went behind my back to side with the enemy, that was her only question? Angry, I put the cup down, the tea splashing over the rim. If I had wanted questions without advice, I'd have gone to Frank to work through my feelings.

"That's all you have to say? I need—"

"You're a whirlwind of emotion. Since we met, you have been a pillar of control. For the first time, I am seeing a woman spiraling. I have no advice for this woman. I do not know her."

If Gregory were here, he'd roll his calm along my skin. The last time we met in the park, he had spoken about my emotions and my inability to access them. Without so many words, he believed the source of my abilities might have reached a self-imposed wall. Perhaps it was the tea or the sudden realization my emotions were out of control, but I imagined the walls building around me brick by brick.

Claudette's hand shot out, grabbing my arm. "No, child. Walls only mean to divide ourselves into smaller facets. Process your feelings, yes, but do not run from them. The time for running has ended."

Had she just agreed with Gregory? Did they both know something I had yet to try? I hardly felt powerful at that moment. My mind was scattered and focusing on anything other than the swirl of information had me scared. Even a psychic can have moments when the future feels uncertain, malleable, and willing to progress as I didn't matter.

I held back the wave of emotion gripping my chest. Between breaths, a flash of a carousel appeared, silent and unmoving. I shook my head, unsure if the image had been anything more than a distant memory. I caught sight of two men chasing a kid. Unlike the others, the vision came and went without fuss, leaving me to deal with the weight bearing down on my chest.

Tears formed in the corner of my eyes. No, the woman who stormed into a warehouse to stop the mob had wilted away. Claudette stood, wrapping her arms around me. I kept it together for so long. But as she cradled my head against her breast, I lost control.

I sobbed.

Chapter Twenty-Seven

1942

Like Edward, the world moved around Olivia. Without a whisper, men answered her every whim. A hearse had carted away the body. Where people should have raised an eyebrow or gasped at the sight of a man wheeling a body, nobody reacted. Even Edward hadn't shown the skill to render himself all but invisible.

I studied Olivia as she moved through the lobby. I sought a gap in her armor. As we passed through the lobby, people continued about their business. Her jaw tightened. She thought nobody would notice the slight stagger in her step. I squared off against an opponent I had never fought; I made sure to note every potential advantage.

Catherine however didn't bask in her abilities like her counterpart. There was no flying through the lobby or suitcases being dragged behind us by an invisible tether. Her abilities were more straightforward, an invisible hand extending from her body and doing her bidding. I watched her levitate this morning, but could she fly? Did she have limitations with what could be moved? I assumed it was like any muscle.

I tried to stop doing that, assuming. It would get me killed. Right now, I needed to study and take away every bit of information I could while I waited to uncover their true motives. Even if everything in my gut was wrong, and they were truly trying to make the world a better place, there was the matter of the men in bomber jackets. They thought themselves safe, untouchable by these henchmen. They hadn't watched a mentalist attempt to influence one only to find himself on the wrong end of a switchblade.

"Edward," I took him by the hand, more than a little aware of the ring firmly placed on his hand. "Stay with them."

"You suddenly trust Olivia?"

"Heaven's no. But I can't imagine there are many places safer than being surrounded by more mentalists. I just…" I struggled with the words. "Don't take her offer, at least not yet." I whispered the word, waiting until Olivia and Catherine reached the exit of the hotel lobby. I wanted a moment alone with my fiancé. Even without her within earshot, I still feared she could infiltrate our conversation. The thought of somebody poking about my mind left me more than a little uneasy.

"There is safety in numbers, but I don't want to see you indebted to them. I mean, what do we really know about them?"

He turned to stand between me and the door. His hands started on my arms and worked their way up until they softly held the sides of my face. The thumb of his left hand stroked my cheek, causing me to lean into his hand. He stared long enough, his eyes studying me with a hint of admiration. I started to feel self-conscious.

"I know you don't trust Olivia."

"It's not that I don't trust her. There are too many questions that are going unasked. And the ones she answers, how can I believe her?"

"You have to have faith." Edward wanted me to believe. He wanted my blessing that this was a good move for him. I hadn't had the time to process the ramifications. While I donned a mask and stopped muggers, could Edward be seizing an opportunity to change the world for the better? A sense of hypocrisy suddenly washed over me.

"Edward, what if you joined me?"

His eyebrow lifted. The simple motion softened his features as he sorted the meaning behind my words. Did normal couples have our issues? Our dates consisted of debates on the hierarchy of mankind. We had sex in the most unexpected locations in New York. Then, just to cement our bond, we survived serial killers. But despite all these radical relationship experiences, I found it comforting to see they hadn't hardened him. Underneath the man with ambition hid the boy I loved.

"You mean, your night time hobby?"

I nodded. "We've talked about it before. You're not losing me. If I don't do this, I'll regret not knowing the impact I could make on the world."

He leaned in, kissing my forehead. Did he sense my worry? Gregory would have pushed back, pushing a calming breeze through my body.

Edward talked about the future as if it hadn't already been written. The words started in my throat and they rested on my tongue. I wanted to tell him, to confess the one secret that could change our relationship. If he knew about my abilities, he'd understand that the future wasn't something I feared. We could speak in certainties and there wouldn't be a regret of the choices we made. As the words touched my lips, I pushed aside the fear of how this could demolish our relationship.

Then I saw her staring through the window. Olivia.

I bit back the words, swallowing the life-changing phrase as if it were a dry piece of bread.

"What if I said it was me or them?"

I spoke the words, but they were unlike me. I didn't like some of Edward's choices, but I had never thought to change his views with an ultimatum. If I could steer him away from a path that led to him bleeding in my lap, I'd push my luck. But as the words hung in the air, a tightness pulled at something deep in my body.

"Eleanor Valentine." The words were soft, quiet. He spoke them as if they had access directly to the part of me that remained rational. Edward had never seen me be vulnerable, not like this. Unable to read my thoughts, he was the one needing reassurances of what I thought about us. Me, I knew the immediate timeline of our romance.

"I love you," he whispered the phrase. The boy I loved was alive and well, determined to squash my fears. "Tonight you'll protect the streets," the tightness traveled up until it gripped at my heart. I knew the words were coming, "and I'll take the first step toward protecting all of New York. Eleanor, together, we can change the world."

Had it been an ultimatum, I'd have lost.

I would have been content. I'd have returned to accepting his ambition and determination to rise above mankind. With a glance over his shoulder, Olivia's smile stretched from ear to ear. I wanted nothing more than hear her scream as brass knuckles knocked teeth free of that perfect smile.

"You know I love you," I said.

"I never doubted it," he kissed me again on the forehead.

The tables had turned. Edward found himself secure in our relationship. He turned to follow Olivia. A black car had pulled up to the curb, and the driver opened the door for her. With a brief glance over his shoulder, he gave me one last wink before climbing in alongside Olivia and Catherine.

The door to the car shut, and I feared it was an omen, a sign. As the hearse departed, passing in the background, housing Gregory's body, a chill ran through my body. I shivered, wondering if this was a sign from Claudette's angels.

No, it hadn't been an ultimatum. But why did I feel as if I lost?

Chapter Twenty-Eight

1942

I had seen glimpses of the carousel in Central Park. In the middle of the night, any passerby would think me crazy for sitting on the park bench in the dark. Not so long ago, Edward had sat beside me devouring his Penny Sunday while we laughed. The memory happened before the Society entered our lives. We were both misunderstood, alone, and desperately craving the comfort of being near another mentalist.

For being able to see the future, I hadn't seen it leading me to a fiancé. While people worried about their tomorrows, I always thought far beyond the point of my death. I had seen metal atrocities tear through a museum and a winged woman leaping from roofs. Did living in the future mean I didn't appreciate today as much as I should?

I smiled. Edward had picked out the horse for me to ride on the carousel based on the dress I wore when we first met. The look of worry laced with excitement on his face had been the moment I fell in love.

"I'm going to be annoyed if a vision brought me here to go down memory lane." I enjoyed remembering life before wearing a mask and stopping mobsters. We were no longer those people. Fate had complicated our lives and here I sat ready to drill my fists into the face of some wrongdoer.

The hour passed as I waited on the bench. The leather jacket warded away the cool night, but eventually, the cold found its way into the sleeves. I couldn't stay still any longer. I strolled along the path toward the amusement park ride, curious to see if I could spot the horse Edward had chosen. Even with the moon hanging in the sky, it was impossible to make out the colors. I'd have to drag him here again so we could relive a simpler time.

"I can have the money for you next week."

Trouble. Two men, in trench coats, gathered around a tall, lanky gentleman. It wasn't the challenge I hoped for, but I didn't care. If I wanted more skulls to crack, I'd venture toward Hell's Kitchen and find more men in need of a beating.

"That's not how this works," the shorter of the trench coat wearers drove his knuckles into the man's torso. I had no idea why these men were in the park in the middle of the night, but the vision had led me here. Twice now, I had pinpointed my place in their timeline. It was progress. I would have to tell Greg—

The empty feeling flooded with anger. My left hand dug into my pocket, grinding the charcoal until it coated my fingers. While I swiped it over my eyes, the second man took a sucker punch, knocking their victim to the pavement. No, not a victim, just another low-life who made a series of bad choices. I didn't hurry as I tied the mask about my face.

Eleanor, I'm trying not to intrude, but it's hard to ignore the anger.

Edward's voice didn't diminish the heat pushing itself through my limbs. My right hand slid into my pocket. The brass knuckles had become like a second skin. They allowed me to feel each blow as I dispensed my brand of justice. The thought of Gregory lying still in the bed and the cold eyes of Olivia had me tightening my grip.

I need to get this out of my system.

"Hey," I shouted. "How about somebody who fights back?"

"It's her," the shorter man said to his companion.

I wondered who had shared the tale of the masked woman? There was a satisfaction in knowing my reputation continued to grow. The scum who roamed the city at night should know there was always a chance they'd encounter me. Fear, I wanted them to experience fear at the sight of me.

Eleanor.

He spoke my name with such a force I had a moment where I saw the world through his eyes. Olivia and Catherine both wore white robes and his arms were covered in white fabric. Whatever they burned in the room reminded me of Claudette's shop, earthy, with a hint of wet grass.

The man on the ground turned over. There was no way to make out his features, but I hoped they gave away his shock. I wanted the goons to know a woman had beaten them. But I wanted the victim to know, too. Nobody here was innocent. They all needed to witness the vigilante justice.

Neither of the goons approached me. They were smart to wait and see my plan of attack. They had heard enough to know I was dangerous. But little, helpless me, how could I be as dangerous as the rumors had said? I walked directly toward the man on the right. I could stop him with a single surprise blow, but I wanted a fight. If this was going to be the only one tonight, I'd give them a chance.

The roof of the building was surrounded in flower pots filled with red roses. One moment I was preparing to trade blows with two men, and the next I stood atop a building similar to my own apartment.

After a few seconds, I realized it was my building. Except there was no Susan Lee hanging over the ledge, brazenly smoking her cigarettes. The moon had gone from a quarter to full in a split second. Had it been the first time, I might have gasped at the change of scenery. But after Edward transported our minds throughout New York City, I had grown accustomed to the shock of the white room.

"Where are you?" He could only summon me if he were here. I might have feared Olivia pulling this stunt, but the thousands of red roses, that was the opulence only achieved by a man.

"Edward, I was about to beat the snot out of two low lives. I don't want to rush whatever this is, but I think my attention should be with the thugs."

Time didn't flow the same in the white room as it did in the real world. I experienced a similar shift when I summoned the ghosts. I didn't move faster than the rest of the world, but my brain, it moved at the speed of light. The white room was the same. We could spend hours here for only a few fleeting seconds to pass in reality.

While I had only known Edward for six months. We had already spent what seemed to be years together. I knew him well, even if it was this fantasy version of him.

"I didn't quite like how our engagement progressed last night."

The voice had no origin, no physical body speaking. Edward was everywhere, watching my reactions even if I couldn't see a manifestation of him. I hated when he did this. I chided him for trying too hard to pretend he had something in common with God.

"Edward, I don't have time for this. And neither do you. Aren't you in the middle of, what did Olivia call it? An initiation?"

"We can do both. Together, but apart."

The moon shone brighter, making the sea of red roses appear even more vibrant. I was about to yell, to scream obscenities. I raised my fist in the air to threaten him when I caught the side of the white lace sleeve wrapped about my arm. I froze, inspecting the exquisite stitching. I had seen this dress before, one of Emma Jean's creations in the store the day I first met her.

"Edward, what are you getting at?"

Then started the violins.

I was standing atop the roof. No, I was next to the carousel. There was a damp chill in the air and the smell of roses. I knew Edward could multitask while in the white room, but I had never found myself in a situation to attempt the feat. I marveled at the concentration necessary to exist in two places at the same time.

There was something intoxicating about the experience. I led a dual life. During the day I hid, wearing the mask of normalcy. At night, under the cloak of a dimly lit sky, I removed the mask, finding myself one deed at a time.

I gasped at the thought.

"Edward, do you see yourself as somebody else around them? Like you're hiding?"

"The dame is crazy."

I almost didn't see the drawn back fist. The man didn't turn his body, putting his weight into the blow. In the gym, that sloppy approach had cost many neophytes their first match. Catching a fist before it can hit you isn't as easy as one might think. Without the help of the ghosts, I'd have most likely missed the kidney punch. It might not be easy, but it was impressive to all who witnessed.

His partner in crime froze. To him, I must have either blocked the punch or refused to flinch from the blow. For a moment, he glanced over his shoulder. I hoped he didn't consider running. I hated when the bad guys ran. There's no satisfaction in beating a man who runs away and cries when you crush the bridge of his nose.

The hand yanked out of my grip. Both men tightened their fists. No, they would not run. Add that mistake to the list of bad choices they made this evening.

"I don't care what you are…"

"I've never seen Eleanor Bouvier in a mask." A moment ago, he had been nothing but an omnipotent voice speaking. The man stepped from the rows of red roses as if emerging from an invisible doorway.

The man had appeared dashing last night. But nothing prepared me for the tuxedo. He opted for the cummerbund, a wise choice. He handed me a single perfect rose. Even though I knew none of it was real, as I held the flower to my nose, I could smell the rich velvety scent.

"I don't have the words to explain it," his cheeks darkened under the moonlight. "But I have never met a woman who demands the world see who she is. No, I don't think you've hidden behind a mask. No. But perhaps you are discovering the Eleanor you always were?"

Our relationship was a language Edward had to learn. Most of his life he didn't need to trust and guess the intentions of the surrounding people. That changed when Skippy found him. But I had to assume Edward didn't seek a romantic affair with the mentalist. Edward learned to be vulnerable, to speak about his insecurities. Between the two of us, I wasn't the emotional one.

"Dammit, Edward." I fanned my face. "You've gone and made me get teary-eyed."

He left the buttons to his jacket open, showing just how well the white dress shirt hugged his frame. His hands slid into his pockets, pushed back the bottom of the coat. I gasped.

"I'm not just a pretty face."

Holding up my arm, I let my eyes adjust to the white lace.

Under the moon it might be difficult to tell, but the white room defied the laws of the universe. The light intensified. Lace decorated my arms, all the way down the bodice and along the train of my dress, it had been dyed the softest of baby blues. The cummerbund wrapped about his waist matched.

"Edward Valentine," my voice cracked. I choked back the tears.

"Eleanor Bouvier, would you do me the honor?"

His reach was superior to mine, at least my arms. Spinning on my left, I used my upper body as a counterbalance, drilling the heel of my boot into his sternum.

"Oomph."

He buckled over, trying to cough but unable to catch his breath. Koji's tactics were unheard of in a fair fight. It made it even more fun to watch them scramble to figure out how to attack a woman willing to kick.

I brought my foot back, using my arms to drag my body into a spin. I had never attempted the move. But after watching Koji use it on me day after a day, I improvised. To finish the spin, I raised my left foot. My heel struck the spot where his head connected to his neck.

It didn't knock him down. I didn't slow, bringing my hands high over my head. Forming a club, I jumped up, slamming my fists onto his back. The man dropped without so much as a spit of air.

His companion decided it was time to intercede. Skilled fighters worked in tandem, leveraging their numbers to tackle a fighter like lions herding a zebra. These were not seasoned fighters. The fight could be over in seconds, but I wanted to drag out the event.

He pulled back his right fist, preparing to throw his entire body into a right hook. I ducked. He wasn't hopeless as he shifted, attempting to reverse the strike and drive his elbow into my jaw. I blocked with my forearm, using my left fist to strike him in the kidney.

"You, bitch."

Trench coats were the least practical garment in a fight. Even a dress could be torn to make lateral steps easier. But a trench coat, it was like wearing a weapon with endless possibilities. I grabbed the back of his coat, pulling it over his head. He tried to stop me, but now he flailed blindly.

"Didn't your Momma teach you to respect women?"

Yes, it was immature taunting.

The first man wrapped his arms around my chest, trapping my arms. I tried knocking the back of my head against his nose, but found the man too tall for me to reach. There were so many options to hurt the man, I needed to pick the most satisfying method to inflict pain.

I grabbed his pinky finger. While he tried to squeeze the breath from my lungs, I bent the digit back until it snapped. For a second, he loosened his grip. I let him grab me again, squeezing me so his fingers were tucked away from my grasp.

"This is going to hurt." I wanted him to fear the next two seconds before I rendered him a blithering mess.

He extended his arm with a slight bow. The pots filled with countless rosebushes parted. A red runner lay the length of the aisle. At the end, on the opposite side of the roof, a trellis covered in vines was backlit by a full moon.

When I presented Edward with Frank's ring, I assumed we'd finished with the formalities of marriage. It appeared as if my would-be husband required more of a traditional ceremony. Of course, it happened in a place only attainable by mentalists. Our lives would never be normal, but we persisted at bridging the gap between our worlds.

I accepted his invite, linking my right arm with his left. Olivia and Catherine flashed in front of my face. The room had been lit entirely in candles and casting shadows across their white garments. Just as I traded blows with muggers in the park, Edward partook in an extracurricular activity.

"You're being initiated?" I didn't want to ruin the moment, but I needed to know if the vision had been true.

"I am. You're saving an innocent soul?"

"He's not so innocent, but yes."

He led me to the start of the aisle. The violin music shifted. Even I recognized Pachelbel Canon in D Major. It wasn't my taste in music, but it held just enough elegance for the imagery Edward had mustered.

"I know this isn't exactly—"

"Edward, it's perfect." We took our time moving down the aisle.

"I never imagined I'd meet a woman like you."

I kept my eyes forward, eyeing the rooftop altar. "The feeling is mutual. Edward," I cleared my throat, worried I'd trip over my need to explain just how much he meant.

"Yes?"

"There was a time at the hospital where I wanted to die. I thought about suicide, but I couldn't bring myself to do it. I wanted the doctor to take the choice out of my hands."

"You wanted them to kill you?"

I nodded. "I know it sounds foolish."

"It doesn't sound foolish at all." He let his arm drop, sliding his hand into mine. He clasped it as we walked toward the altar.

"The doctor nearly killed me. I went without struggling and at the last minute, I couldn't let him do it. He tried to rob me of my choices. I can't explain it, not with words. But if I died, I wanted it to be by my hand."

He didn't interject or ask questions. We reached the end of the carpet and stood in front of the trellis. We turned, facing one another. His free hand hovered in the air, waiting for me. He crossed the gap between us, taking my hand and pulling me close. With a kiss on my forehead, I stared into his eyes.

"Frank rescued me that night. But the truth is, I've wondered night after night if I would change the outcome."

"Eleanor—"

"No," I tightened my grip on his hands. "Was I strong because I wanted to live? Or weak because I didn't want to die? I've thought about that question for years. But," I let go of his hand and held the sides of his face. "But I've stopped asking that question. I no longer regret living."

I had never shared these words with another person. Frank knew about my submitting to the doctor that night. But he didn't know that guilt seeped from every pore since. Part of me had continued to wonder if the world would be better had I died in the hospital basement. I had never spoken it aloud until now.

"I'm glad to hear that." He leaned his head to one side, kissing the spot where my hand connected to my wrist.

"Because I have something to live for."

He didn't recoil as I drove the heel of my boots along the top of his feet. He cursed, squeezing me tighter. I appreciated that he didn't let go; it made it easier when your opponent stayed within easy reach. I didn't need to prove that I was the better fighter. As I stepped to the side, pulling my body askew to his, I knew my ranking.

I slammed my fist back, connecting with his manhood. I continued driving the heel of my fist upward, ramming his testicles inside his body. He let go, falling backward as he cradled his boys. I wasn't allowed to play dirty in the ring. But here, fairness had no place in the scuffles without referees.

Unless he had a gun, he wouldn't be a problem tonight. His partner, however, he pulled the trench coat off his arms, throwing it to the ground. There was cursing and threats about showing me what a "real" man was capable of. Neither of these goons were man enough to handle me.

"Let's do this." I raised my guard, fists balled in front of my face. I narrowed my stance, putting my left foot forward. Boxing had become second nature, but I struggled to remind my body to include Koji's teachings. I relaxed the fist on my left hand, maintain my grip on the knuckles with my right.

Predictable. He charged in, his right fist drawn back so far there was nothing he could do but throw the punch. I let it get close before I thrust my left hand against his forearm, redirecting the blow so it passed harmlessly. He had to scurry, almost tripping over his own feet as he spun about to meet me face to face.

"Fight me," he growled.

"It's more fun taunting you."

It was the truth.

He didn't rush, instead he measured his steps as he approached. His left hand should protect his face, but it dipped low. The man hadn't spent time at the gym. Frank would have him doing push-ups each time he lowered his guard.

His right fist feigned a jab. Even if he struck me, the angle would have made it a weak attempt. His shoulder pulled back, and I readied myself. I could have summoned the ghosts and slowed time. I could have predicted every thrust, but tonight I needed to prove I wasn't limited by these gifts.

Leaning into the punch, he thought his mastery of misdirection had me at a disadvantage. It sped toward my face, and I ducked to the left. His arm hung in the air as he missed. I hooked my right wrist on his forearm and punched his elbow with my left. The snap of bone reverberated down his arm and into my hand. He howled while I savored the permanent damage.

When he pulled away as I snaked my foot behind him. He tripped, tumbling backward, trying to protect his arm from smacking the cement. Kicking with his feet, he tried to put distance between us. When he saw there was no way he could outrun me, he tried slamming his toes into my stomach.

Clutching the man's foot, I spun about, straddling the leg. With a swift turn, the pop cut through the chilly evening air. Dislocating the man's hip might not kill the man, but it'd make it near impossible for him to go out in the evening to torture New Yorkers. I brought up my foot, ready to smash it down on his manhood, leaving him in as much pain as his partner.

The man, consumed in his wailing, didn't fight me off as I got on my knees straddling his chest. I opened my fist, letting the brass knuckles fall into place before tightening my grip. The howling turned to sobbing as I pulled him up by his collar. His bravado vanished, bested by his opponent.

The walls between the park and the white room thinned as violins filled the night air. My senses struggled to separate the two. Here I held a man, ready to shatter his jaw while there, I held the hands of my beloved.

"You're pathetic." I drew back my fist. One strike and I'd knock several of his teeth loose.

"Please, please, please." He begged.

The priest stepped out of emptiness between the trellis'. Something about his face struck me as familiar. It wasn't until I thought of pasta that I realized the man wasn't a priest at all. He had been the waiter at our favorite restaurant. The chuckling started, and I had to commend Edward on his creative solutions.

"Our waiter?"

"Their sauce is as close to God as I can imagine. It seemed fitting."

"I have to agree with you. I'll never be able to look at him again without laughing."

In the other direction, down the aisle we had walked, there were several chairs. While their features weren't perfect, he manifested versions of Frank, Claudette, and Susan Lee. He worked hard to make sure this was the fantasy I always wanted. But it wasn't those in attendance that struck me. Sitting in the front row were three empty chairs. I didn't need to ask to know who they were meant for.

"Edward…" He knew me well.

"I didn't want to make presumptions." I appreciated that he didn't conjure their likeness. It was enough to know they held a permanent spot in my life, even if they couldn't partake directly.

The priest cleared his throat, signaling that the ceremony was about to begin. Despite the pomp and circumstance, I expected at any moment he'd ask us if we wanted more fresh garlic bread. Much like the question posed by the priest, the answer would always be yes.

The ceremony didn't last more than a minute before we reached the historic moment that would change my life.

"Do you, Eleanor Bouvier, take this man to be your lawfully wedded husband?"

Edward knew Susan Lee well enough to include her sobbing hysterics as part of the background. She held a handkerchief to her face, smudging her makeup as she wiped away tears. Frank put his arm around the woman, holding her while she waited for my answer.

She waved me off, reminding me to focus on the question at hand.

"I do." I did. Being Eleanor had been a period of my life wrought with pain and loss. I imagined with those two words, the page turned and we started a new chapter. No longer would I be that scared girl on the farm.

"And do you, Edward Valentine, take this woman—"

"I do." Eager. His cheeks turned red as he jumped the gun. He held both of my hands, giving them a gentle squeezing. Neither of us had any intention of getting married. Fate accelerated our time table. As my thumb ran along the ring, I smiled. Masterfully, I had cheated death. No, I wouldn't hold Edward as the grim reaper collected his toll.

"It is with the power of..." he mumbled, and I snorted as the replica faltered, "I pronounce you husband and wife. You may—"

Edward pulled me close, wrapping his hand behind my waist. He pressed his lips against mine. His kiss was urgent, intense, and anything but chaste. Had Frank been present, I'd have had to pull away from embarrassment. But here I returned the kiss, my arms wrapped around his neck.

He rested his forehead against mine. Gently swaying as I spoke. "May we have a long and prosperous life together?"

"Who knows what the future holds for us?"

I knew. Fate would not take this man.

A loud gasp had me staring at their victim and the sheer horror written across his face. There was no need to fear the men, not with the broken bones and... he wasn't scared of them. I let go of the goon's leg, taking inventory of the damage I had inflicted.

"What are you?" he asked, getting to his feet. "You almost killed them."

Had he not gasped, I might have done just that. I stepped back, fighting off the smell of roses.

I danced on the line between vigilante and criminal. The knuckles struck the pavement with a ringing. I had trained to change the city, and I found myself dangerously close to becoming the very thing I fought against.

Even without the ghosts, I found the power seductive, whispering in my ear. If I continued, neither of these men would ever be a threat again. Releasing them, they could return to the streets and run amok. My black and white point of view bled gray.

The goon continued sputtering, begging for mercy. I picked up the knuckles and slid them into my pocket. I didn't care what they thought of me. But the man I tried to save, scurrying back as I walked closer to him, that threatened to break something in me.

"You're safe," I said.

"From them or you?"

Chapter Twenty-Nine

1942

The rain mirrored my dreadful mood. It stopped being individual droplets and appeared to come from the sky in sheets. The wind had started howling earlier that evening. For the last several blocks, I was the only person foolish enough to be outside. Water made its way down the street like a river, sloshing over the curb, leaving my shoes filled with water.

I stopped for a moment, taking inventory. If I was going to meet Olivia, I wouldn't be doing it without suitable weapons. There was only one knife in the holster, a problem from hurling the blades and then not being unable to retrieve them. The brass knuckles tucked in my right pocket. But most important was the gift from Frank. On my left wrist, a brown strap held a man's watch. The seconds ticked past, each one existing and dying before my very eyes.

Twenty-two minutes to go.

The row houses were all similar, building after building joined at the hip. At the front of each, stairs came down from the front door, leading to the tiniest of courtyards. It was obvious it was the nicer part of New York. Apartments were a dime a dozen, but having even a four-square foot patch of grass, that showed money. The fence was decorative. A low wrought-iron fence pretending to keep intruders at bay.

Olivia had summoned me. A simple word breaking through my defenses. *Come.* In that statement she had buried a location. I wasn't entirely sure I had the right street. It felt like I was growing closer. I did not like the fact she had invaded my mind, nor did I care for her placing information in my head. How I longed for the simple use of a telephone to connect with another human.

The number on the door flashed in my mind and something assured me this was the correct address. I debated staying in the cold, refusing the woman's summons. Only yesterday morning had she disposed of a body like it was taking out the trash. Nothing about the woman said safe or welcoming. Housed within those walls was a game of chess, filled with false moves, trickery, and subterfuge. At least out here, my biggest concern was a runny nose and a cold.

"Edward, I pray we survive this."

I reached for the gate, fingers wrapped around the wet metal. The visions bombarded me, like the television flipping channels. Images of soldiers dying in a war. The victory parade as they returned. The blinding light consuming a city. And lastly, New York in ruins.

Do come in, Eleanor.

The whispers of her voice held an indifferent tone. I shivered as I pushed open the gate. Climbing the steps, I had no idea what awaited me on the inside. Did the woman stand in the foyer, knife ready to lunge? No, Olivia wouldn't be so crass, she'd come at me when I least expected it, when she believed I was the most vulnerable. Unfortunately for her, I hadn't been surprised by the future since I was a young girl.

The door seemed off, darker than the others on the street. I'm sure there was a psychological reason behind the choice.

Did I dread dealing with the woman? No, I wasn't scared by her, not in the least. After dispatching Bertolucci and his men, I had faith in my abilities. This time, however, I feared that if I called out to Edward, it might not be me he sided with. *That* scared me.

I opened the door, waiting for Olivia to reveal herself. The interior was lit by a large chandelier, almost as tall as me. The stairs spiraled until it reached a balcony on the second floor, open for those to see the foyer below. For a small-town girl from the Midwest, I somehow found myself in the presence of money more than not. My apartment would almost have fit in the foyer. If I didn't know better, I'd believe that money beseeched the corrupted.

"Hello?"

I eyed the last step, a small six-inch rise until I stood within the building. Cautious, I crossed the threshold. Bathed in the chandelier light, I heard the low trumpet of a jazz musician playing. If I walked into another ball or party, I might have to hurl myself through a window. The need for people with money displaying their wealth wore on me.

"Olivia?" I whispered the name. The room held entry into a parlor on the left, and a living room on the right. A narrow hallway led to the back of the building, where I assumed the kitchen lived. Unlike the doctor's brownstone, I could only describe the decor here as sanitary. The study's floor had a white rug with white chairs. I couldn't imagine the care needed to maintain their pristine crisp lack of color. But everywhere, the rooms were filled with white and gray, with a single splash of color in a painting or a table runner. The woman had tastes that ran opposite to the common definition of decadent.

I had seen these colors before. In visions of the future, people decorated their homes with accents of color. It reminded me of the room where I died. Far into the future, the room held a similar palette. I shook the image from my head, trying to focus on the present.

"Olivia, I grow tired of your games." There was no point in being friendly. The woman had summoned me and playing coy was nothing less than cowardice.

"This isn't a game, dear."

In the study, the woman wore a red dress. The attention-grabbing color matched her personality. Olivia didn't strike me as the type of woman with any level of subtlety. Even the manner in which she walked accentuated her hips. No, Olivia craved the attention from all in a room. I couldn't imagine her being anymore my opposite.

"I suspect everything you do is part of a game."

She rested her hands on the back of a chair. The stark white of the fabric made her skin appear even more radiant. Had she picked every piece in this room to flaunt herself? I had no doubt that Olivia put care into placing everything, from the chairs, to the side tables, to the glasses on the drink trolley.

"I suppose you are right. But what part of life isn't a game?" Olivia got under my skin simply by existing. "The question is, what game are we playing? You have your games. I mean," she let a chuckle slip, "you go into the evening hoping to rid the world of bad guys."

"New York is my home. I won't let scum—"

"You get defensive. That's not my intent, not at all. You are doing admirable work. If you don't believe me, that's on you. But a woman standing against unquestionable odds, and persevering night after night, you have my respect."

Of all the repartee I expected this evening, garnering the woman's admiration had not crossed my mind. Had I read her wrong? Frank often said not to snap to judgment about people. However, my gut instincts were rarely wrong.

"Eleanor Valentine," I forgot the woman only knew me as

Edward's fiancé. "Perhaps we can sit. I believe there is much for us to talk about."

"Where are the others? Where's Edward?"

The smug grin vanished. The air in the room grew heavy, and I suspected the answer would be almost as diabolical as I feared.

Olivia came forward, closing the distance between us. My muscles tensed, fear at any moment I'd see the flash of a blade. I prepared to summon the ghosts, to toss her against a wall and pound my fists against her face until I couldn't tell where the blood ended and the fabric began.

"I summoned you here, because of Edward."

"What did you do to him?"

"Him?" There was no crafted visage, no stern upper lip, or distant eyes. The accusation shocked the woman. "Eleanor," for the first time, I sensed fear in her voice.

"Your fiancé is a killer."

Chapter Thirty

1942

The fire crackled loudly. Each pop reminded me of mobster gunfire. I had spent so much time imagining the flame in my head; I had forgotten how beautiful it could be. Bits of white turned yellow, then orange and red before it repeated. It was mesmerizing, so much so I nearly forgot Olivia sat opposite of me.

I had been ignoring her for the better part of ten minutes. I believed she had offered me a whiskey. Since she spoke the words, proclaiming my husband was a murderer, time stood still and moved too quickly all at once. She may have spoken more, elaborated, but at the moment, I only wanted to hear the pop, pop, pop of the fire.

Beautiful as it is destructive. She eased her way into my mind, softly, apprehensively, as if I might startle. Had she been Gregory, she might have caught hints of sorrow, a bit of sadness, but most of all anger. Not at Edward, but at myself for turning a blind eye. He'd ask me to verbalize them, to give each emotion a name. I had spent years around doctors who presumed to know the inner working of my mind. They boasted degrees that fed their egos.

Gregory didn't need a degree. His wisdom hadn't been learned from a textbook. The man simply listened.

Gregory died.

The compartment where I tucked away my emotions had filled, and now they spilled across my being. I had no filter, no ability to lie. Gregory would have said something pithy, perhaps even inspirational.

"Gregory," I whispered the word, fearful that acknowledging him might summon a true ghost. Olivia stirred the ice in her glass. I hadn't seen her pour a drink. The amber liquid had nearly vanished. Time passed and I couldn't account for seconds. I had been so guarded, so worried Olivia would kill me… I had grown careless.

"He discovered me," Olivia stated as if it explained everything. "He found me almost twenty years ago, living on the streets of London. I had grown cocky with my abilities, and when I tried to liberate his wallet, he put me to sleep. Once upon a time, he was quite the confident man."

I didn't object to the story. I had questions about her accusations, but now, we were two women mourning a man. "When I awoke, I thought he might be a dirty old bastard. Gregory has been nothing but a gentleman. He will be missed."

Missed? I expected her to launch into a story, to explain their relationship. But missed? Olivia might be the only woman more detached from her emotions than me. I couldn't wait to tell Frank. It'd be a banner day.

"You're incredibly cold."

Olivia let out a calculated laugh. "Because I do not mourn death? Think of me what you will, but being part of the Society has taught me many harsh lessons. But their first, life is temporary. I have seen many men perish because of them. I will see plenty more."

"So you simply write him off?"

"Gregory taught me what it meant to be a mentalist. When he

was younger, he wielded his abilities with a controlled ferocity. He was the first of us to stand up to the Society. When he spoke against them, they drugged him and locked him away. It was months before I saw him again. He didn't explain how he escaped their prison, but I knew. Even asleep, he manipulated them. He could have gotten away, but that wasn't his way."

"He came back for you."

Olivia nodded, then took a sip from her glass. She paused for a moment, the glass nearly half empty. I raised an eyebrow as she guzzled the rest. I longed for the sticky bar at Harry's and a bottomless glass of whiskey. Even if I were the only woman there, the stodgy men were at least simple creatures.

"In his old age, Gregory mellowed. But that night, I saw him as the man he used to be. A telepath has limitations. We can control the motor functions, yes, but sifting through an adult brain is like searching for a titleless book in the grandest of libraries. But Gregory, he washed over them like a wave beating against the sand. This reserved man had the heart of a warrior."

"I know."

My words caught her by surprise. She scooted to the end of her chair, placing the tumbler on the drink trolley. "I had my suspicions."

"You did?"

"I touched your mind at the gallery. Your walls slammed into place. I knew then. Gregory had a flair for the dramatic when it came to visualizations. To this day, I still employ the technique, even if there aren't many telepaths to keep at bay."

"I will miss our visits in the park." My already small circle shrunk by one yesterday. The man tolerated even my most annoying habits as he ensured I grasped the limits of my abilities. My heart sunk in my chest as it dawned on me that he'd miss watching them develop.

"Edward." I shook my head. Caught up in my melancholy, I had drifted away from Olivia's earlier proclamation. My mind wandered, scattered and it was difficult to focus. I stared at the whiskey glass in my hand. I tried to push my way through the daze and focus on the woman's accusation.

"You said Edward is a killer," I set the glass on the side table, wanting to give the woman my full attention. "Elaborate."

"Quite simply put, Edward killed Gregory."

"Impossible. He'd never do such a horrible thing."

"Do you say that because you believe it? Or because he is your fiancé?"

Olivia knew exactly how to burrow to the root of my insecurities. I had witnessed Edward do horrible things in the past few days. He had killed Bertolucci without regard. A moment in which I demanded he show restraint. He had not. Had he confessed my apprehensions, or did a supernatural intuition lay out my concerns for her to see?

"Only a telepath can control the Barren. They were given a command to kill Gregory."

"The Society?"

"No," she said firmly. "It is one of the many reasons why they want us under their thumb. No, Gregory's death could only be carried out by a telepath."

"And how do I know it wasn't you?"

"You do not," she said. "Edward is an ambitious man. I can only assume he wanted to cement his position amongst his own kind. With Gregory gone, we are but two. Edward wants to secure the position for himself, and for you."

I shook my head, trying to push away the alcohol. The edges of my memory had grown blurry. I couldn't recall Olivia filling my glass. Had I finished three or four glasses before I put it down? Like Frank, I enjoyed my alcohol, but unlike him, I knew when to say no more. I closed my eyes while attempting to stop the room from spinning.

"You're absolutely sure the Society cannot control the Barren without a telepath? Could they have some other method?"

"I know it's hard to comprehend, but I am sure of this. Edward must be in league with the Society. Perhaps—"

The glass in my hand was more than half full. Despite the liquid sloshing about, I couldn't smell the familiar fragrance of smoke and Pete moss. I held the glass close to my nose, and after a deep inhale, I was sure something was wrong.

"It wasn't the doctor and his wife killing mentalists," I opened my eyes, sneering at Olivia, "was it?"

In her red dress, she stood out against the carpet while she knelt at my feet. Her hands on my thighs were distant. I didn't remember her standing or getting into position in front of me. Hazy memories had little to do with booze. Had she added something to the alcohol before she poured it? Did the glass have arsenic coating the rim? There were too many inconsistencies, and I found my memory unreliable.

"Eleanor, my dear," Olivia's voice was soft, gentle even. She reached up, her hand lifting my chin so that our eyes locked. "One by one, I eliminated the weak. But you," she patted me on the cheek, "are anything but weak, am I not right?"

"You," my words slurred, "underestimate me."

"Do I, Eleanor? Or do I simply know your limitations better than you?"

Gregory had said it best, "I have none."

Chapter Thirty-One

1942

Olivia preyed on my inexperience.

The study in the brownstone had been reconstructed. She considered the tiniest detail, from the bricks of the fireplace to the dark wood of the mantle. Thorough as she might be, the inconsistencies hadn't gone unnoticed. The lack of smell from the whiskey and the perpetual filling of the glass might have slipped past me.

Her mistake had come from the missing minutes. Between the two of us, only I had an intimate love affair with time. I checked the watch. Six minutes.

"No." My voice came across weak, dazed, and hardly more than a whisper. I stared past Olivia to the flames within the fireplace. I summoned my own, calling the part of me that accessed the ghosts.

"No." The sluggish weight in my limbs pushed away. The mind witch had attempted to snake her way into my thoughts, to manipulate me without being seen. If Olivia's ego exhibited a little more patience, perhaps the false sense of security would have succeeded. But she seemed unwilling to wait, and for that, I had to thank her.

"NO!" The scream echoed off the walls, causing the entire room to ripple. Olivia fell backward as if I struck her with my fist. I raised my hands, inspecting the skin along the back of my hand. Droplets of water formed, falling off and vanishing in thin air. A shiver started in my spine and I grew increasingly aware of being cold and damp.

"You're good," I said, looking to the ceiling, hoping for a clue. "You're great, even. But this isn't my first time." I climbed off the chair, not sure what I hoped to find.

"Eleanor, what has gotten into you?"

The library held a collection of antique literary works. I brushed my finger along the spine of a book, startled by the coarse, tightly woven threads. I pulled at the tome and opened it to the middle. Empty. I turned the page and found every page lacked writing. I pulled a second book and found the same.

"A white room."

Olivia was only inches away from me, the smug smile firmly in place. "Edward warned me. He said you were something different."

"You killed Gregory."

Olivia's laugh dripped with condescension. The woman found joy in my confusion. But like any bad guy, her ego required explaining my shortcomings.

"No, dear. Edward killed Gregory," she leaned in as she whispered the final words, "*for* you."

I stepped back, uncomfortable with the idea Edward could kill in cold blood. But it wouldn't be the first time. I had over-looked Bertolucci. But also the wife in the ballroom. Was a lovesick girl turning a blind eye?

"There must always be four," I mumbled.

"He was to be killed after that medicine woman of yours. But he discovered me. I didn't think him capable. Your fiancé has proven himself to know the ins and outs of the city. And then I had the chance to witness your audition."

I raised my eyebrow. How long had Olivia been watching? Taking inventory of my abilities?

"When you killed my precious Barren, I knew you were fit. Edward simply tied off the loose threads. He seems more than willing to finish the battles you begin."

"The mob?"

"I've been told I have issues sharing. New York City might be vast, but I'm not going to stand beside a human. You did me quite the favor that night. I expected it to be more of an irksome task."

I feared that one of Bertolucci's men might assume power, stealing the title of kingpin for themselves. One by one, I eliminated Olivia's only opposition. Just like before, Edward came swooping in, dealing the finishing blow. And with one last dead mobster, I handed the city over to a more terrifying ruler.

"I will ask this only once, Eleanor Valentine. Will you take your rightful position and join us?"

Edward frequently brought me to the white room. Trapped in a tiny apartment in the middle of New York, we escaped all over the city from the comfort of his bed. He conjured images of beaches or cabins deep in the mountains. While lying entwined, we experienced locations otherwise foreign. I had known beauty in the imaginary confines of his mind, but I understood the rules. Conviction bred action. Emotions harnessed correctly could make the other writhe in bliss.

I wanted to scream 'no' at the woman. I wanted to let the rage climb from my stomach and redden my cheeks. It wasn't enough that she asked the question. She believed that part of me wanted to sit on a throne by her side. Did Edward vouch for me? Did the man not understand his wife? I let my nails dig into the book in my hand.

I struck Olivia across the face with the spine of the book. She spun about in the air as if a truck had hit her. Slamming into the bookcase with a thud, she rolled onto her back, staring up from the hardwood floor. With my answer bruising the left side of her face, I understood she wanted this outcome.

"I hoped you'd resist." As if by a supernatural force, she stood upright. In the process, her red dress transformed from an evening gown to a snug suit of armor made of leather. Edward had displayed the same tactic, moving from a tuxedo to a bathing suit depending on the location he chose. Just because I understood the rules of the game, didn't mean I had any natural gift in this simulated reality.

Since Edward first brought me into the white room, I feared it'd reveal my lack of telepathy. I might be a mentalist, but I had taken such great care to hide my secret from him. I had hemmed and hawed, debating on if I should reveal my deepest secret. Each trip from my body, I sealed away my abilities, letting him believe, like him, I was a telepath.

The back of Olivia's hand connected with my face. The force of the blow came like a shock-wave, hurling me above the fireplace mantle. She believed herself more powerful, more talented, and elsewhere, her ego might not serve her well. Here, that confidence struck me like a car.

"Now, we shall see who is the stronger telepath."

Olivia didn't know.

Chapter Thirty-Two

1942

The laughter filled the study, echoing as if we stood in the alley between buildings. I couldn't resist. Olivia had made it clear she was superior in every way. In the provocative manner she dressed, the endless supply of money, and even as a telepath, she claimed victory. She was the best in all of those things. But Olivia thought she knew about all my abilities.

"You are indeed the strongest telepath I know." I pushed myself up from the floor. Grabbing a poker resting next to the fireplace, I tested its weight. "But you're also the most ill-informed person in this room."

"Oh, do tell."

I prepared for the sheer joy. From the moment she introduced herself in the art gallery, I waited to see the smug expression smacked from her face. I anticipated it occurring as I drilled my fist into her face, but I'd gladly watch it happen as I set off an explosion with one sentence.

"I'm not a telepath." Four minutes.

The smirk faltered as her brow furrowed. Not exactly the expression I hoped for, but considering Olivia's control over her emotions, it spoke volumes. It seemed that the intelligence Edward supplied the woman had been painfully under-researched. It goes to show, men only see the facade women put on display.

Now I was going to beat the daylights out of the woman.

I snatched the poker, familiar with the weapon. It was almost identical to the cast iron rod from the doctor's house.

I swung. It struck Olivia on the shoulder, forcing a satisfying scream. I wanted the woman to suffer. First, she'd pay for killing Gregory, then for trying to kill me, and last, for seeding Edward with her infectious ideas of superiority.

The second swipe of the poker struck her across the face. The leather armor did nothing to protect Olivia as blood splattered across the white rug. Olivia clutched the side of her face where her cheek had been cut in two. I cringed at the sight of her teeth through the flaps of skin. With a final thrust, I jammed the poker into her gut, twisting as the tip vanished into the leather.

"Good riddance."

"Who are you speaking to?"

Over my shoulder, Olivia took a sip of whiskey before tossing the glass into the fire. I turned my head slowly, scared to see who squirmed at the end of the poker. Blood speckled his salt and pepper beard. The light in Gregory's eyes dimmed, his thrashing becoming sporadic. He staggered back, collapsing.

I didn't want to admit it. Olivia had bested me. The corpse at my feet was nothing more than a figment of my imagination, but it clarified that sheer might wouldn't win a clash with Olivia, at least not in the white room.

"Oh, Eleanor, your resistance is admirable. But you're here at my beckoning. Be a polite guest and take a seat. Whatever skill you might have, it's no match for a woman of my caliber."

The woman had let the facade falter when I revealed I wasn't a telepath. She let it slip again as she found herself at a loss for words to describe my abilities. Olivia might be a talented telepath, perhaps the most powerful one I had ever met. But I was a precog.

In my mind, the image of the flame exploded outward, blowing apart the barriers I used to shield myself from intrusion. Here, in this space, I could feel the heat as I imagined the fire surrounding my body. Even Olivia paused, unsure of what occurred. Washed in fire, I allowed it to crawl along my skin, absorbing its radiance. In the study, my avatar glowed, and the look of confusion on Olivia's face was as priceless as I had hoped.

"You've never met a mentalist like me." The ghosts found me, even in the white room. Seconds and minutes passed, and I watched every motion of mine and Olivia play out while she remained frozen in time. I returned to the present, wanting her to see, to fear, to be unable to comprehend.

"Tricky," she said, unimpressed. Her hand passed through the face of her own ghost, only seconds into the future. I had, of course, seen the action before she made it. No action would come as a surprise.

"You are a curious creature, indeed."

Olivia stepped forward. A mirror-duplicate separated from the original. She repeated the action until three of her stood shoulder to shoulder. The multiple versions of the telepath were harder to sort, but not impossible. But it wasn't her ghost I wanted, I didn't care about these phantoms.

"I can do the same, my dear. You impress no-one."

I pulled at the fire, reminding myself of the anger. Gregory wanted to break down my walls, to force me to confront emotions long since buried. I recalled the glassy look of his eyes as I closed them. Anguish consumed me, burning as intensely as the flames. His face gave way to Frank's as he handed my mother the letter, and the arm waving through the ice as Benjie drowned.

I cried out in anger.

The first ghost pulled away from me, then the second and then a third. I simultaneously experienced three different versions of the world. They each charged toward a different image of Olivia. I had seen it before, but never had I summoned it on my own. Three versions meant choices. I could pick and choose the future I faced.

From each of the three, hundreds of different timelines spawned. Punches, ducks, dodges. Every action created a new ghost until I struck dozens of Olivias. In many she gained the upper hand, driving her hand into my chest, pounding my face with her knuckles or blowing me across the room as if I weighed nothing. I dismissed the losses and alternative versions arose. In a fraction of a second, I had lost thousands of confrontations and won only one.

I followed my ghost into battle.

Chapter Thirty-Three

1942

I kicked the table, blocking the Olivia on the left. Anger manifested as supernatural abilities. The poker flung from my hands as I willed it forward. The metal sank into the Olivia on the right, pinning her to the wall. I raised my hands into the air and the wood around the fallen woman pulled free, surrounding her like the hand of a golem. While she screamed to be free, I stood face to face with the remaining Olivia. Her face vibrated, the ghosts about her giving away the real woman.

"A novice with a taste of power."

Her insults betrayed her own insecurity. Why did bad guys always insist on speaking so much? What manual did they read that required them to come up with pithy dialogue? I planned on beating the woman to death with that book.

Far from hitting me, Olivia thrust both of her hands forward. The air in the room shuddered as a blast of wind slammed into me. Had I not already seen it, she might have very well flung me across the room and out the front window. But with a simple wave of my hand, the attack redirected, throwing books from the bookshelves.

I retraced the steps of my ghost, following, careful to pick the right path at every fork in the timeline. Thinking me a novice, Olivia's ego might be her most open vulnerability. I wanted to exploit it, to harness her superiority to take her down one peg at a time. She should fear me, and she would.

I spun, thrusting the palm of my hand forward into the emptiness. Power rippled down my arm, a concentration of anger pooling in my palm. Olivia blinked out of sight. She appeared, thinking she surprised me. Anger tore through the room. The walls cracked, and the floor splintered as I unleashed years of repressed pain.

The woman's flesh tore away, shed like a snake's skin. Leaning into the blow, she reached out, struggling to overcome my will. As she peeled away, the woman underneath appeared ragged, less perfect than the Olivia I met in the gallery. Acne scars peppered her cheeks and her hair held less of a sheen. The woman that captivated the crowds was nothing more than a figment of her imagination, a telepathic disguise.

I exhausted myself, and her arm thrust forward, grabbing me by the neck. I clutched at her wrist, aware of the thin scars covering her arms. Even the true Olivia held beauty. It became obvious her insecurities were deeper than I anticipated. For a moment I wondered if she might be a warped reflection of myself, had Frank not rescued me.

"It's not too late," I said.

Olivia screamed. The waves of sound pounded against my face. The pain at the base of my brain pulsed down my spine until even my fingers twitched. The high-pitched screeching in my head threatened to rupture my eardrums. I resisted scratching at my skin, digging away at whatever caused my skin to crawl.

"Keep your pity." I touched upon her deepest fear. A woman consumed with perfection and lording over those in her presence demonstrated her weakness. Olivia clawed her way to the top to exert control over her own life, to ensure she'd never feel power-less again. Try as I might, I pitied the woman.

"If you won't serve me—"

I didn't wait for her to finish. I knew the speech, I had heard a thousand versions of it and each one she ended by threatening me before killing me. This wasn't where I'd die. The ghosts ensured the future and Olivia had yet to realize I had already won this confrontation.

Pulling at her wrist, I wrestled with the woman until her grip loosened. I pushed my fingers through hers, snapping one finger at a time. I turned, reaching for the poker impaling her doppel-gänger. The mirror image was inches from wrapping her fingers around my throat. The poker tore itself from the wall until the bloody metal rested in my hand.

Her double fell to the ground, and I raised the poker high in the air, ready to drive it through Olivia's eye. The room broke apart, shaking as walls fell, revealing the infinite space of the white room. I didn't blink, focused on the prize.

"You have no idea who you've fucked with." Two minutes.

Olivia stopped holding back. The rage of the woman slammed against me, threatening to knock me back. I endured, determined to see this confrontation reach its end. Nothing of the study remained. We stood upon emptiness, Olivia continued screaming at the top of her lungs. I wanted this to end, to see the woman die by hand, to know that I hadn't handed New York to a viler evil than the mob.

The screaming stopped and Olivia's eyes softened. That pompous grin returned to her face, certain she had found the limit of my conviction. "You can't do it, can you, Mrs. Valentine?"

I had seen the possibilities, the endless outcomes. If I left her and walked away, she'd retaliate. There was no alternative other than killing the woman. I had seen the future, many futures, and only one of them resulted in a corpse at my feet.

I thrust, focusing my anger, my desperate need to change the world. The poker penetrated her left eye, and I shoved with all my might. The back of her skull exploded as it pushed through. For a moment, I hated what I had become, but given the options, I'd shoulder the burden. For the future of my city, I would not let her Society prevail.

Olivia fell backward. Dead.

Even in the nothing, the blood from her head pooled, creating the idea of a floor beneath us. The poker pointed straight up in its new home. I couldn't help but pant, exhausted by the swirling emotions. I hadn't believed it possible, but when push came to shove, I beat Olivia at her own game.

Hovering over the corpse, her flayed skin filled out, returning to nothing. I noted the smug expression, her signature look. Even with the glamour and telepathic makeup washed away, she remained a stunning woman. But the smirk, that condescending expression, that would haunt me as I fell asleep.

I froze.

A speckle of red splashed along Olivia's cheek as I stood over her body. First one, then two more followed. Just north of my navel, a red stain spread across my blouse. Touching the red, my mind struggled to understand what had happened. I coated my fingers in blood, *my* blood.

"I warned you, Mrs. Valentine."

Appearing thousands of miles away, Olivia stood at an open door. In her hand she clutched a kitchen knife, half the blade buried into an identical version of myself.

"Never believe a fight only has one front."

I looked down at Olivia's hand. She gave the knife a slight twist. While I mercilessly slayed the telepath in the white room, she had sought to take the fight into the physical realm. And just like that, I could feel the rain again, beating at my back as I stood in the brownstone's doorway. My mind faltered, trying to understand what had happened and how I stood here despite being in the study.

“It wasn’t real,” I whispered.

“I commend you.” Olivia’s damned smirk. “But you’re out of your league.”

Just as I predicted, my vision came true.

Time had run out.

Chapter Thirty-Four

1942

Olivia stood in the doorway, barring me from entering the foyer. One hand rested on the back of my head, fingers entwined in my hair. She held me firm and for a moment I thought we'd kiss. Emotion filled her once cold and detached eyes. I reached for her throat, as a pain seared through my torso. Clutching her shoulder, my knees threatened to give out.

I glanced at the watch on my wrist. The hour hand held firm at twelve and the minute hand was two minutes until midnight.

"I only ask once."

With a slight turn of her wrist, something in my body screamed. With my free hand, I grabbed her arm. She pulled at my hair, forcing our eyes to meet. It wasn't enough to kill me, it wasn't enough to run me through with a kitchen knife. She wanted to watch the only person between her and victory, die.

"I," speaking hurt. The air in my lungs ignited like they were filled with fire. On my wrist, I eyed Frank's watch, noting the exact time. I forced a smirk, an act of defiance, and not my last. "I saw this."

Screaming, I slammed my head against Olivia's nose. I

grabbed her hand around the knife, easing it out. It was difficult to tell if it hurt more or less. There was no end to the pain, just new fresh waves, unyielding, refusing to let me focus.

You bi—

I jabbed her in the throat. My limbs were growing heavy, and I feared if I looked down to see the blood pumping from the wound, I'd go into shock. I stepped from the doorway, grasping the railing. Slick with water, I staggered, slipping and half falling down the stairs until I reached the bottom.

My body wanted to surrender, to lie back and close my eyes as the rain pelted my forehead. The ghosts walked along the street, ignorant of my hemorrhaging. I fought to stay conscious, looking for the ghost who might whisk me away from this world. I couldn't be certain how far into the future they revealed… until I saw him.

A man in an army uniform ignored everything but me. At first, I couldn't be sure, with the rain in my eyes. The uniform blurred. It wasn't until I saw the young boy standing at his side I…

"Poppa," I whispered.

Angels stood amongst the ghosts, and the tension in my body relaxed. For a moment, it seemed as if the pain receded. My brain knew shock had set in. Poppa wrapped his arm around Benjie's shoulders, and I wasn't sure I cared if death took me. My father's head shook back and forth. He wasn't ready to accept me, not yet.

A screeching filled the air as a car passed through their ghosts. The taxi door opened, and I heard a panicked voice screaming for help. They lifted my body and with the slam of the door, I could tell we were moving.

"Eleanor, what happened?"

"Did somebody shoot her? Is… okay? Does she… hospital?"

The buttons of my jacket were torn off. I moved in and out of consciousness. Words, I could hear them, but only some of them made sense. I had nearly drifted off when I heard fabric being torn and a sudden pressure pushing down on my abdomen. I shrieked, barely sounding human.

"Stay with me, Ellie."

Benjie called me Ellie.

"Stay with me!"

I coughed, grimacing at the pain. My eyes opened. Blood covered Susan Lee's face as she bit into a piece of fabric from her shirt, tearing off a chunk. She balled the fabric, put it on the wound and placed my hands on top of it.

"Mercy or New York General?" asked a man's voice.

She repeated Claudette's address. I put my hand on her arm, squeezing it the best I could.

"Ma'am, are you sure?"

"Just do it."

She balled a jacket under my head, trying to make me comfortable. Even in a crisis, her bedside manner persevered. She lifted my hand for a moment and then returned to holding the bandage in place. I hadn't wanted her ever crossing into my world, but there were few people I trusted with my life like I did Susan Lee.

I wanted to check the watch, but I couldn't raise my arms. The effort of speaking forced a hiss through clenched teeth.

"Susan Lee," the words came out in a gurgle, "you're late."

Time had no meaning. Coming from a precog, the phrase was almost humorous. There was shouting, followed by the sweet smells of Claudette's shop. Bright lights flashed in and out. Pain took hold until the world seemed to disappear.

Scrapes and bruises hadn't prepared me for teetering on the line between life and death. The lights of the room flashed on and off, and I didn't know if each time my eyelids closed if this was the moment death would claim me. Having seen my demise, I feared this might be the moment in which destiny collaborated with fate and shook on a truce. The irony, if this was the moment I finally cheated the universe.

The afterlife had the smell of morning dew, a scent I hadn't smelled in years. On the front porch of the farm, I gazed at the endless fields of wheat. When the sun broke, the world would ignite in a blaze of gold, but for now, only the sky closest to the horizon had lightened to a vibrant blue.

I hadn't thought of my childhood home in ages. Standing on the front porch, I rocked on the board Poppa promised he'd someday fix. There had always been a more important project before he left one last time. I pressed my foot on the wood and it creaked. Was this heaven? Locked away in a childhood memory, would I spend the rest of eternity surrounded by my first home?

Moving along the road, a cloud of dust filled the air. The engine of the neighbor's truck roared as it grew closer. I held onto one of the columns, holding the roof in place. I held my breath, waiting for the truck to arrive. Holding my breath, I could only hope that this heaven wasn't built for one.

The truck didn't stop, instead passing by the house. With the honk of the horn, a shadowy figure inside waved. My heart sunk, worried that this might not be heaven at all. Would I suffer, hopeful for the sight of a familiar face, but never seeing them? It seemed appropriate that the afterlife would be just as cruel. I tried. So close to making a difference, only to fail.

"You haven't failed."

The deep tone of his voice filled my heart. I didn't dare turn. I couldn't bear to hear his voice, but not see him. There was no way I'd allow myself to fall for trickery again.

"I saw you," I whispered, "on the street, with Benjie."

Even as the screen door opened, I refused to believe he might be there. Instead of slamming shut like when I or Benjie went running outside, he let it close slowly. His boots caused the boards to creak, and at any moment he'd be standing next to me.

I fought tears, refusing to accept that I might see him one last time.

"No," I said.

The hand rested on my shoulder. I lost the fight as I reached up, resting my fingers on his. The coarse skin was a welcome home. I couldn't hold back as I turned. Even as an adult, he stood nearly a foot taller than me. He hadn't shaved for days. Momma would refuse to kiss him until he cleaned the dark stubble from around his lips.

"Poppa," I clutched the man. My arms reached around, tightly squeezing him as I laid my head on his chest. The smell of sweat and earth permeated his button-down shirt. I didn't care if any of it was real. My senses were on fire and each of them assured me this was my father.

I had forgotten the feel of him patting my head, stroking my hair. When the dreams turned to nightmares, he sat on the edge of my bed, brushing my hair until I fell asleep. I feared I had forgotten his face, and as I pulled back, tears filling my eyes, I found myself thankful. Each line at the corner of his eyes, the slight bend of his nose and the bald line through his eyebrows, they were all there.

"We saw you, Ellie. We've been watching this whole time."

"Benjie," I cried. I wanted to beg for forgiveness. There were no words to describe how sorry I was for not protecting his only son. I didn't know where to begin.

His hand grazed my cheek. "I know. He doesn't blame you. Neither do I."

I squeezed his rough hand, savoring the calluses along his fingers. "I'm so sorry."

"You can't change the past." The man chuckled. He didn't laugh often, not a real belly laugh. It was easy to detect when he found something funny, this was more of an ironic humor to see him through a bad situation. "I guess the past isn't for you. Is it?"

Poppa had been the first to believe, to truly accept that I

wasn't a child with a wild imagination. Without that, I believe I would have lost myself those first few weeks in the hospital. I clung to his assurances. I wish I could have told him that.

"In the hospital—"

"Shhh," he whispered. "For a woman able to see the future, you spend an awful lot of time thinking about the past."

I raised an eyebrow. I wanted him to be real. If this was heaven, we could spend eternity together, tending to the fields. I knew better. Too good to be true, this wasn't heaven. Even if I found myself wrapped in a fever dream, at least I recalled my father's face.

"Has Frank been a good father?" His voice sounded heavy, curiosity mixed with the sadness of missing out on every milestone. I wanted to tell him everything, to share every high and low.

"Yeah. But he's not you. He never replaced you." Tears welled up in my eyes, before trickling down my cheek. I wanted him to know he'd always be Poppa.

"I'm not worried. You were a handful. You're still a handful. I'm glad you've found a new family." He rested his hands on my cheeks, wiping away the tears with his thumbs.

"Does he make you happy?"

I scrunched up my face like a child offered a healthy snack. "Frank?"

"Ellie," the tone turned stern, "I think you know who I mean."

"Edward. He's ..." I searched for a word that made sense. I grew so comfortable with the lies, I forgot the few people who understood all of me. "He's like me, Poppa. He can read minds."

His head slowly shook back and forth. "That's not what I asked, Ellie."

Last night had been magical. It was the fairytale wedding every young girl hoped for. We stood across from one another, confessing our love. In everything but paperwork, I had become

Eleanor P. Valentine. Had it been before I listened to Olivia taint my memories of Edward, I would have said absolutely.

"I do." It was true. He made me happy more than not.

"But..."

Had it been Poppa, Frank, or even Susan Lee, I would have said I had no doubts about our relationship. But Olivia's words had struck a chord, burrowing beneath my certainties.

"I love him. But I don't think I trust him."

The words stung. They had lingered for some time, but I thought if I buried them beneath my day-to-day, they'd go away. Had Susan Lee spoke those words, I'd have told her to lose his number and move on. She was worth more than a man who put his own ambitions above her.

In the presence of Poppa, I felt like a little girl again. "It hurts," I confessed. He pulled me in tight, holding together my broken pieces with a bear hug.

"Forward, Ellie. Your destiny has always been ahead of you."

"I've made so many mistakes." Edward, Olivia, Gregory—the monumental daunting sense of dread seeped into every ounce of my being. I had a mission when I took on the mob. Now, for the first time since Frank rescued me, I thought of myself as the victim.

"You'll make plenty more. Knowing what's coming doesn't make you perfect."

"If I can't change the future—"

"You can." If this was a dream, then my father was nothing more than a garble of memories and my own personality. "Perhaps not yet. But you will."

"The Society. They ..." I didn't know how to voice the emotion hanging over me. "They won."

His hands held onto the side of my face, his thumbs rubbing my cheeks. His eyes shimmered as the sun crested over the horizon. I wanted this moment to continue, to go on forever. I might dwell on the past, but at least it was comfortable, familiar. Part of me admitted the constant fighting had taken its toll.

"You don't believe that." He brought me in for a hug, cradling me in his arms, giving me a sense of security. "No matter what they call you, no matter the names you take, you'll always be Eleanor Paula Bouvier. And I know my daughter," he leaned down and kissed the top of my head, "and she's a fighter."

The pressure along my arms faded away. I grasped at the ghost of my father. Nothing remained but the smell of earth and a farmer's determination. I didn't care if any of this was real. For too long I dwelled on the farewell robbed from me. It was enough, a memory of the valiant, duty-bound human I aspired to be.

I sat on the stairs leading from the porch. The light from the sun worked its way across the yard, inching its way to my feet and along my legs. His words echoed loudly. So much had gone wrong, and even in the face of giving up, some part of me refused to succumb to the machinations of a band of mentalists. The light warmed my torso. I gazed along the golds of the wheat field, remembering the sensation of running my hands along the top as Benjie chased me through the fields.

"Thanks, Poppa," I whispered. Looking forward, staring into the brightness of the sun, I found a renewed determination. Blinded by the sun, I couldn't give up, this wouldn't be the end.

"I'm a fighter."

Chapter Thirty-Five

1942

"I have a heartbeat," screamed a voice.

"Lebaga has delivered her," said another voice.

The shadow of a person, a woman with her hair hanging down along my face blocked the white light. My eyes adjusted and I could see the tear-filled face of Susan Lee. She held my face in her hands, squeezing enough to force my face on hers.

"She's awake," Susan Lee's voice was a mix of disbelief and thanks.

"There's nothing more we can do, except pray."

I couldn't make out Claudette, just a blurry form in her shape. I listened as she slid the tools of her trade onto a metal tray. Susan Lee clutched my hand, leaning in and kissing my forehead. She mirrored my father's motions. Her hands, unlike his rough skin, were soft to the touch.

I tried to speak, but neither my lungs nor my voice cooperated. Susan Lee let her thumb pass back and forth over my knuckles. I didn't want her caught up in this madness. She didn't deserve to be part of a life of secrets and mentalists. The walls

231

that separated aspects of my life fell away. I feared for my dearest friend.

She leaned in close, whispering in my ear. "Whoever did this, they'll pay. I promise you, Eleanor."

Yes. Yes, they would.

- The End -

Visit RemyFlagg.com
for More Children of Nostradamus

About the Author

Jeremy Flagg is the creator of the dystopian superhero universe, CHILDREN OF NOSTRADAMUS. Taking his love of pop culture and comic books, he focuses on fast paced, action packed novels with complex characters and contemporary themes. He continues developing the universe with the Journal of Madison Walker, an ongoing serial set two hundred years in the future.

Jeremy spends most of his time at his desk writing snarky books. When he gets a moment away from writing, he binges too much Netflix and Hulu and reads too many comic books. Jeremy, a Maine native, resides in Charlotte, North Carolina and can be found in local coffee shops pounding away at the keyboard.